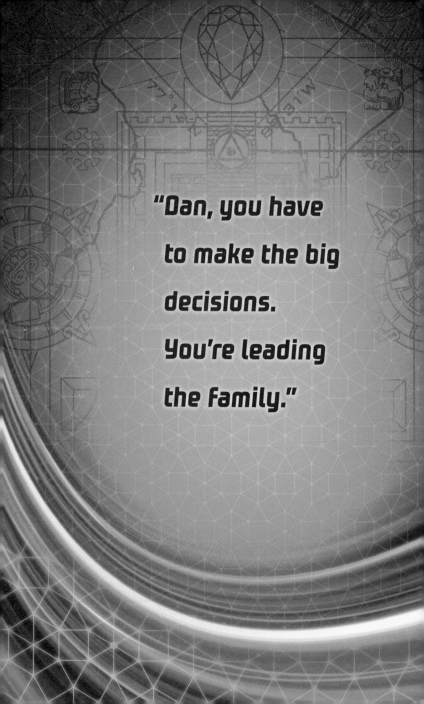

"Dan, you have to make the big decisions. You're leading the family."

UNSTOPPABLE

COUNTDOWN

THE 39 CLUES

NATALIE STANDIFORD

SCHOLASTIC INC.

For Secret Agent Willard Standiford
in recognition of his outstanding work in the field

Library of Congress Control Number: 2013951101

ISBN 978-0-545-52145-1

10 9 8 7 6 5 4 3 2 1   14 15 16 17 18/0

Candice Starling p. 65: © Ryan Jorgensen—Jorgo/Shutterstock; Young Starling p. 65:
© Val Lawless/Shutterstock; Mural p. 109: Photograph "Jugadores" © Justin Kerr.
Book design and illustrations by Charice Silverman

First edition, May 2014

Printed in China 62

Scholastic US: 557 Broadway • New York, NY 10012
Scholastic Canada: 604 King Street West • Toronto, ON M5V 1E1
Scholastic New Zealand Limited: Private Bag 94407 • Greenmount, Manukau 2141
Scholastic UK Ltd.: Euston House • 24 Eversholt Street • London NW1 1DB

MIX
Paper from
responsible sources
FSC
www.fsc.org   FSC™ C020056

PROLOGUE

London, England

J. Rutherford Pierce watched the queen of England carefully as he made his way down the endless receiving line. First the prime minister of Australia, then a British pop star, now a French actress . . . The queen smiled, nodded, shook hands, and made small talk with each one of them, over and over and over again while photographers recorded every gesture. Pierce waited for his moment, his turn in the spotlight.

Of course, as the head of Founders Media he controlled most of the newspapers and TV stations, so he made sure his tour was the top story every day. But he had to give the reporters something to report, and that was the fun part. That was where he got to be creative. He might look like any handsome, superfit mogul touring Europe before announcing his candidacy for president of the United States, but his movie-star smile blinded the masses to the truth: With every stare, he was planting seeds for his masterpiece—world war.

With his wife, Debi Ann, at his side—sweet, quiet, helmet-haired Debi Ann—he'd managed to alienate every European leader he'd met.

So far.

When he and Debi Ann finally reached the head of the line, the queen smiled and nodded at him just as she had to everyone else. Debi Ann lit up like a child on Christmas and gave the queen a deep curtsy.

Curse Debi Ann. He'd clearly instructed her not to curtsy. British subjects were required to curtsy before the queen, but Americans were not—though curtsying was encouraged and every other woman at the reception had done it. The plan was for Debi Ann to defiantly refuse to curtsy to a monarch. But she couldn't even handle that simple instruction.

Twenty minutes later, the pomp and circumstance was over and he and Debi Ann were seated at a tea table with the queen. He picked up his teacup. It was so delicate, made of fine bone china, white trimmed with gold, from the seventeen hundreds. Priceless, he thought. His mind couldn't help calculating the value of everything around him.

And then, once again, it struck him—that odd, annoying tremor. His fingers shook ever so slightly, and he couldn't control them. It was worse than the last time, in Spain, when his left leg shook visibly enough that he had to sit down to hide it, mystifying and conveniently insulting the Spanish king.

The tremor jolted his hand and he dropped the price-less china cup. *Crash!* Tea splashed over the antique carpet and the cup shattered against the leg of the queen's chair. A few droplets of tea dotted her pale blue silk pump.

At the sound of trouble, the photographers swarmed. They snapped pictures of Pierce, the broken cup, the stained carpet, the queen's annoyed expression. It flashed over her face for only an instant, but they caught it. He'd flustered her, broken her practiced composure.

It could have been a disaster. But Pierce's quicksilver mind calculated a way to turn this mishap to his favor.

These days, everything seemed to go in his favor. Funny how that worked.

"Sorry there, ma'am," Pierce said, putting on a homespun American accent.

"Don't worry, it's quite all right," the queen assured him coldly.

Pierce was accosted by reporters on leaving the palace.

"What happened with the teacup?"

"Was the queen upset that you broke her china?"

"Will this affect US-British relations?"

"The queen didn't look happy, did she?" Pierce jested with the press. "Well, I'm sorry if one of the richest women in the world was upset over one little teacup, but if you ask me, I did her a favor. Did you see how old that china was? I think it's about time she got some new dishes."

The joke hit its mark. The reporters laughed, and that night Pierce's quip was all over the international news. AMERICAN BUSINESSMAN TELLS IT LIKE IT IS, one headline read. J. RUTHERFORD PIERCE'S WORKING-CLASS BACKGROUND SHOWS, said another.

That "working-class background" was completely made up, of course. Pierce had expanded his father's newspaper company into a global conglomerate, but he hadn't exactly started out with nothing.

"Back in the States, Mr. Pierce's supporters are watching this European tour and cheering him on," an anchor reported. The film showed a group of Americans wearing tricorne hats, carrying signs that said PATRIOTISTS FOR PIERCE and WE DON'T NEED NO STINKIN' TEA!

It was all a lot of background noise, a smoke screen to cover up his real goal: to be the most powerful man in the world.

The tremors worried him, yes. But he would find a way to fix them. Only one thing truly stood in his way. Or, to put it differently, two kids. Amy and Dan Cahill.

They couldn't stop him. No one could. But Pierce was not a man who liked loose ends.

The Cahills are my final obstacle, he thought. *But not for long. Because soon they'll be dead.*

CHAPTER 1

Guatemala City, Guatemala

Amy Cahill put on her sunglasses in preparation for a paparazzi mob scene as the plane landed at La Aurora International Airport, but all looked quiet. Funny. This should have helped Amy relax, but she'd forgotten how to do that. Instead, the nerves in her neck tensed even more.

She and the others — her brother, Dan; his friend Atticus; and Atticus's older brother, Jake — deplaned and walked through the airport toward the gate where they would board a chartered helicopter. They'd hired a local pilot who knew how to fly through the volcanic jungle mountains, since landing at Tikal was tricky.

"Nice and quiet," Jake said. "For a change." People — normal-looking people in the tourist uniform of shorts, sandals, and T-shirts — sat playing with their mobile phones, walked calmly to their gates, gazed in boredom at the same old duty-free chocolates that seemed to be for sale at every airport.

Amy didn't answer. There was nothing to add to Jake's observation other than: *For now.* Or: *We'll see.*

Besides, she doubted he'd meant the comment for her. He was barely speaking to her, communicating on an as-needed basis. The same went for Dan. Atticus slipped up occasionally and offered her gum or flashed her his sweet smile, but then Dan would glare at Att to chastise him for the small betrayal.

Amy told herself it didn't matter if they hated her. She wasn't racing around the world to make friends. As the leader of the Cahill family, she had to make hard choices — like leaving Dan, Atticus, and Jake behind when she headed to the Arctic Circle alone. Abandoning the few people she loved had felt like cutting off her own hand, but that didn't matter. She had a job to do. As long as the others didn't get in her way, whether they included her in their jokes and gum-sharing was their business.

There was a shout from a newsstand and Amy turned toward it.

"There they are!"

"The paps at two o'clock," Dan muttered. A small mob of photographers zeroed in on them, their gear clanking as they ran.

Amy couldn't contain an exasperated sigh. *Here we go again.*

It was bad enough that J. Rutherford Pierce sent murderous thugs after Amy and Dan wherever they went. On top of that, he'd ensured that the paparazzi was obsessed with them—*Amy and Dan Cahill, the teenage leaders of the richest and most powerful family the world has ever known.* The source of their power was a serum that Pierce had managed to steal, enhancing his own power and making him exceedingly dangerous. Amy and Dan were on a desperate mission to find the antidote to that serum, and had come to Guatemala because they suspected the next ingredient they needed—"riven crystal," whatever that was—was hidden in the ancient Mayan ruins of Tikal. But it was next to impossible to conduct a covert operation—or even to hide—when reporters publicized your every move.

"That way." Jake pointed to a door marked VIP LOUNGE, manned by a guard.

Amy flashed a VIP Travel Club ID at the guard and they ducked inside, but not before one of the photographers spotted them and took some quick shots. The flash cast eerie shadows on the wall in front of her. She couldn't let the photographers follow them to their waiting chopper. If the paparazzi found out where they were headed, that meant Pierce would know, too.

"Amy!" the photographer called. "Using your privilege to avoid the public? What are we, the unwashed hordes?" Amy ignored him and kept running, but the photog pushed past the guard, who couldn't stop a whole mob determined to get around him.

Amy, Jake, Dan, and Atticus raced through the lounge, dodging placid passengers sipping drinks. Amy leaped over a side table just as a woman reached for her coffee cup. The woman glared at her and snapped, "Rude children!" The comment bounced off Amy's Teflon shell. The days when Amy cared about good manners were long gone. Her near-fatal trip to Svalbard had iced over what remained of her heart. Being hounded by the press could do that to a person—and being hunted by a powerful, ruthless killer, even more. Pierce hardly needed his army to find the Cahills—the press did that job for him.

Dan found a door at the back of the lounge and threw it open. "In here!"

The others followed him through a staff changing area. They ran past a flight attendant shrugging into his uniform jacket. "Hey! What are you—?"

No time to hear the rest of that question. They ran past a long mirror, where another flight attendant spritzed his hair with spray. Amy got a faceful, wiped the spray from her eyes, and kept running without missing a beat.

They found another exit and made their way through the maze of the airport, leaping over suitcases and the legs of people sitting on the floor, until they ended up at baggage claim. A crowd of passengers had just arrived to pick up their luggage. "Try to get lost in the crowd," Amy said. Even if the boys weren't speaking to her, they couldn't block out her orders.

They wove their way among the tired passengers impatient for their bags. Amy heard a shout from the edge of the crowd.

"There's Amy!"

"Let us through!" The telltale flash of lightbulbs popped from across the large hall. The paparazzi had spotted them.

"What are you doing in Guatemala, Amy?" a reporter shouted over the crowd. "Planning to spoil the rain forest?"

"Dan, you following orders like a good boy?"

Amy risked a glance at Dan, knowing that remark had hit a sore spot. "I don't want them to know where we're going," Amy told the others. "We've got to leave the airport for a while. The chopper will just have to wait."

"While we do what?" Jake demanded.

"I haven't gotten that far yet."

Amy led them through a corridor to the airport exit, her eyes scouring the terminal for some other way to get out. But the airport exit was blocked by a wall of six big, muscular, stone-faced men in black suits. Amy knew them all too well by now.

Pierce's men. The soldiers of the Founders Media army.

They homed in on the Cahills, muscles rippling, like tigers preparing to spring for the kill.

"Back!" Amy shouted to the others. "Back the way we came!"

Trapped between the muscle and the paparazzi, Amy would rather take on the paps. Pierce's soldiers couldn't be seen attacking kids. Amy knew Pierce's men had orders to kill, but it had to look like an accident. As they backtracked into the baggage hall, there was a loud buzz and flashing yellow light, and one of the luggage carousels began to spin. Suitcases started spilling out and riding around the conveyer belt. The passengers crowded around, eagerly waiting to grab their bags, temporarily blocking the paps from reaching the Cahills.

"This way!" Dan jumped on the carousel and rode it to the end, disappearing behind a rubber mat. Amy, Jake, and Atticus slipped through the crowd and jumped on the conveyer belt before the paparazzi could reach them.

"Get down!" Amy grabbed Atticus and the two of them hid behind a large red suitcase held together with twine. Someone reached for the suitcase and pulled it off the conveyer, suddenly exposing Amy and Att.

"Hey!" the man shouted in shock when they were revealed. "There are kids riding this thing!"

Amy grabbed Att's hand and jumped off the belt into the center of the conveyer ring. An airport security guard stepped onto the edge of the conveyer to grab them, but one of Pierce's men shoved him aside. Amy could see the crowd parting as Pierce's soldiers surged forward.

Amy, Atticus, and Jake ran and jumped back onto the circling belt behind a big box that hadn't been claimed. One of the men grabbed Atticus's arm and yanked him off.

"Let go!" Jake jumped up, kicking the man swiftly in the chest. The man reeled, knocking the soldier behind him over. They stumbled, tripping over luggage and landing in a heap on the floor.

Amy ducked as a rubber mat swept over their heads, knocking Att's glasses askew. Dan waited for them on the other side as they were dumped out into a secure luggage area and tumbled down a ramp. It was like streaking down a very lumpy slide. Airport workers stared at them in shock and then erupted into a clamor of angry Spanish.

"Don't worry, dudes, we're out of here," Dan said.

Amy glanced back. One of Pierce's men came through the flap, but an airport security guard dragged him back. Security couldn't hold him for long, she knew. "Gate Seven. Move it," she told the others.

They ran past carts piled with luggage, out onto the tarmac. Six of Pierce's men emerged from the luggage area, scanned the tarmac, and pointed in their direction. "Where's our chopper?" Jake asked Amy.

Amy nodded at a helicopter revving up on the tarmac. "That's it up ahead."

"We're not going to make it!" Atticus cried.

Atticus was right. Pierce's thugs had taken a small dose of the serum, and their super-enhanced bodies could run faster than the kids ever could. Without that chemical advantage, the kids had no chance in a flat-out race.

Amy and the others charged for the chopper, but she could feel the men closing in, a hundred yards behind her, fifty, twenty . . . their footsteps pounding, louder and louder, each step sounding of doom.

CHAPTER 2

Amy could almost feel the soldiers' hot breath on her neck — it had a certain odor, a kind of green kale smell mixed with chlorine and ammonia. She knew that smell all too well by now, from far too many run-ins with brick-like men who were trying to kill her.

She turned, preparing to fight. There were five men, four kids . . . outmanned and out-muscled, but if they were smart they might have a chance at escape. She spotted two airport mechanics inspecting a plane about a hundred feet away. Maybe if she could get their attention, the soldiers would be afraid to attack.

She jumped up, waving and shouting, "Hey!" as one of Pierce's men leaped for her. She ducked and let him sail over her, landing with a thud on the runway. Just then a loaded luggage truck zoomed out of the terminal, heading for a jet waiting on the tarmac.

"Jump on!" Amy shouted. She leaped onto the truck as it passed, hiding behind the mountain of suitcases. She reached for Atticus's hand to haul him up after her, but it was slick with sweat and slipped through her fingers.

He ran, panting, to keep up with the racing truck. She grabbed hold of his wrist this time and yanked him up so hard she nearly dislocated his shoulder.

Jake and Dan hauled themselves over the side at the last second.

Amy looked back to see how much ground they'd gained, but Pierce's men kept coming, not far behind the speeding truck. They had no time to spare. She waved frantically at the pilot of their helicopter, who was sitting at the controls. "Let's go!" she shouted at him. "Now!"

The chopper motor roared to life, and the rotors began to turn, slowly at first, then faster. The driver popped open the door.

"Jump!" Amy called to Jake, Dan, and Atticus. "Now!" She took Att's hand as they hopped off the speeding luggage truck. Amy landed on her knees and rolled over the hot tarmac. She pulled Atticus to his feet and ran for the chopper, Jake and Dan right behind them. Pierce's men were closing in. Amy and Dan scrambled aboard the helicopter. Jake pushed Atticus on, jumped in, and shut the door as the rotors whirred faster and the chopper lifted off.

The pilot yelled something at them in Spanish, and Jake yelled something back at him. "He's asking why those big men are chasing four kids," Jake translated. "I told him to just get us out of here." The pilot bellowed again, pointing at the tarmac just below. One of the thugs was leaping into the air, freakishly high, trying

COUNTDOWN

13

to grab the landing skid. He barely missed, tumbling to the ground unhurt as the chopper rose out of his reach.

Amy breathed a quick sigh of relief.

"Thank goodness goons can't fly," Dan said. "Not even serum-enhanced goons."

The boys settled into their seats behind the pilot and buckled up for the ride to Tikal. It was a big helicopter with two rows of three seats facing each other behind an enclosed two-seat cockpit. Amy poked her head into the cockpit to make sure the pilot knew where they were going and to thank him for his quick thinking.

"My pleasure," he said in a thick accent, nodding but not meeting her eye. "Please sit down and buckle your seat belt, miss. The ride to Tikal can be bumpy. We'll be flying over active volcanoes."

Amy sat down and buckled up. Something was bothering her; something about the pilot didn't look right. His torso was thick and lumpy under his jacket. "Did you notice anything strange about the pilot?" she whispered to Dan.

"Like what?" he asked coldly, as if it took super-human effort just to respond to her.

"Never mind." Amy pressed her forehead against the window, frustrated.

The helicopter rose and left Guatemala City behind. Far below, a blanket of brown volcanic mountains rippled.

She shifted her leather bag to the floor and heard a tiny *clink*. She couldn't resist another glance at Dan, who was now engrossed in a computer game. His straight brown hair fell into his eyes, and he had to keep reaching up to sweep it out of his way. Amy tried to stifle a surge of tenderness for him, but the sight was enough to make her heart sting like skin recovering from frostbite. It sometimes was easy to forget that he was only thirteen. If they were still in Attleboro, the biggest thing they'd be fighting about would be haircuts and homework, arguments she'd likely lose because Dan was the most stubborn person she'd ever met.

No wonder they were barely speaking to each other.

Dan was sick of the whole Cahill thing. "I'm out," he'd told her. Once they finally took down Pierce, no more Cahill stuff for him. He planned to disappear and live out the rest of his life quietly and anonymously, with as little mystery, action, and adventure as he could manage.

Amy remembered a time, not so long ago, when Dan would have dismissed a life like that as boring. That's the kind of damage the Clue hunt had done to him. A boy whose life had been so stressful he was ready to retire at thirteen.

Atticus sat next to Dan, his wiry body curled in his seat, poring over Olivia's Codex, his older brother, Jake, beside him, reading over his shoulder. He'd been fixated on a page of weird, unfamiliar glyphs that he couldn't figure out. They were lined up in neat rows, each one a rounded square with a design inside, and between each one was a set of letters and numbers.

Amy had looked at the symbols but couldn't make much of them. Sometimes she saw something that looked like a face or a tongue or a monster. Sometimes they were just dots and lines and circles, almost decorative. They were complex shapes, not letters, exactly, but almost like rough drawings . . . though of what?

They had left the seat next to Amy empty. No one wanted to sit next to her. Jake least of all. Her heart cramped as the ghost of her cruel lie echoed in her head. *I don't love you. . . . You think there's this thing between us, but there never was, and there never will be.*

They didn't understand what it was like, being in charge. They didn't know how it felt to send someone you love off on a mission so dangerous that death was nearly certain. She refused to be the reason her little brother never got another haircut. One more mishap, and she'd be staring at his shaggy brown hair against the lining of a casket. From now on, she'd do what was necessary to keep her family — and the world — safe from Pierce.

If that makes them angry, then too bad. She'd rather have them angry and alive than dead. She put her backpack under her seat and heard the *clink* again. It had been made by a small flask of Cahill serum. No one knew she had it. She hated the idea of having a full, undiluted dose of the serum near her. It was like keeping something radioactive next to your skin, like Superman carrying around Kryptonite.

Atticus was working on decoding the formula from Olivia Cahill's Codex. Lately he'd been obsessed with a recipe in the book for "Crystal Sugar Candy." "If you want some candy so badly, Atticus, I'll buy you some when we land," Amy joked, mostly to try to jolt one of them into acknowledging her presence.

"It's not that," Atticus said. "Rock crystal candy is very simple to make. This recipe is ridiculously complicated. There's something else going on here."

"Crystal . . ." Amy mused. "Maybe there's a connection to riven crystal."

"Maybe," Dan said. "But what *is* riven crystal?"

"Read the description again, Jake," Amy said.

Atticus handed the Codex to Jake. Olivia's description of the crystal was written in Latin, and Amy's Latin was poor-to-nonexistent.

Amy's phone buzzed. "Finally," she said with relief. They'd been out of cell range and out of touch with their base in Attleboro for several hours, and it made her nervous. "It's Ian. Hang on a sec, Jake."

She could sense Jake stiffening from across the aisle and caught the annoyance—or was it anger?—that flashed across his face.

"Ian?"

"Amy."

"It's good to hear your voice."

"Yes, we've been trying to reach you since you left US airspace," Ian said. "Did you make the chopper we set up for you?"

"Yes." No point in going into how they'd barely made it out of the airport alive. "Thanks for your help, Ian."

Out of the corner of her eye she could swear she saw Jake wrinkle his nose and mutter, "Thanks for your help, Ian" under his breath. *Typical.* Jake could barely *look* at her without grimacing, yet watching her talk to a boy she'd once had a crush on turned him from dark and brooding into prickly and childish.

"How's Ian?" Jake asked when she got off the phone. He straightened his spine, buttoning the top button of his shirt and sticking his nose into the air. "Tip-top shape, I hope?" he added in a terrible, exaggerated British accent. "All's jolly well in old Attleboro, is it? Or as I call it, Yankee Purgatory? I do hope I'll be able to leave this blasted land of rubes and return to civilization one of these days."

Dan and Atticus snickered in their seats. Amy crossed her arms, annoyed. "Just read me Olivia's description of the ingredient, please."

"I say, it says here that she used flakes of a riven crystal chipped off a stone from a Mayan temple in Tikal." Jake was still using his fake Ian accent.

"Thank you. You can drop the accent now."

"Jolly good. Funny, I thought you liked British accents."

"Jake—"

"My mistake."

"Yes. It *is* your mistake. What else does Olivia say? In your regular accent, please."

Jake frowned at the book. "Basically, Olivia looked at the rock under a magnifying glass and saw that its crystals had an unusual zigzag structure, as if it had been deformed by some great pressure."

"That sounds like shocked quartz. I saw it on *Weird But True*," Dan said. "It's found in places where nuclear devices have been set off, but also in places where a meteor crashed to earth."

"Chicxulub!" Atticus said.

"Gesundheit," Dan said back.

"No, the Chicxulub crater," Atticus continued. "A meteor hit the earth there about sixty-five million years ago. It caused giant tsunamis and sent up so much dust it almost caused an artificial ice age — like a nuclear winter. Some scientists think that meteor is responsible for the extinction of the dinosaurs."

"I'm a fan of the volcanic theory myself," Dan chimed. "That volcano dust wiped them out."

"Whatever, a meteor landed there," Atticus said. "They've found shocked quartz in that spot, deformed by the impact of the meteor. But it's in the Yucatán, in Mexico, not in Guatemala."

"The Maya traded all over Central America," Jake said. "They could easily have traded for stones from the Yucatán."

"If all we need is a piece of shocked quartz, we can buy it off the Internet," Dan said. "We don't need to fly all the way to Guatemala."

"The book specifically calls for a 'riven crystal from

Tikal,'" Jake said. "It must have some special properties."

"Did the Maya build temples out of it?" Dan asked.

"I checked into that," Amy replied. She was grateful that, at least when they were discussing the antidote, the others dropped the silent treatment. "The temples are built of local limestone. But they might have put special stones at the altars of the temples, maybe something they traded for, something unique."

Tikal was a national park and archaeological treasure. The ruins of a great ancient city—a fallen empire—had been hidden by centuries of jungle growth, but in 1956 archaeologists began to excavate and were amazed at what they found: whole cities made of stone, huge Mayan pyramids and temples, miles and miles of ancient buildings.

"Just as I thought," Atticus announced, waving the paper he'd been using to decode the candy recipe.

"It won't make candy?" Dan asked.

"Not unless you like candy so hard it will break your teeth," Atticus said. "It's a coded message. Sugar, or sucrose, has a chemical formula of $C_{12}H_{22}O_{11}$, but when I decoded this ingredient list, the formula for 'sugar' reads SiO_2. That's the chemical formula for quartz. But it goes on to describe a molecular structure that's a little off, not quite right for quartz. Once I applied the molecular structure for riven quartz to the code, I figured it out. The antidote requires a special piece of riven rock, which has certain molecular properties. One of those special pieces is embedded in the ruins of a Mayan temple in Tikal. The piece Olivia used was broken off from that crystal."

"But Tikal is *full* of ruined temples," Amy said.

"And it's gigantic," Jake added. "How will we know which temple holds the crystal we need?"

"Let me have the book back, Jake," Atticus said. He opened it to the page covered with weird glyphs.

"Check it out." Dan nodded at the window. "That volcano is spewing ash."

Just then the chopper blew through a brief black cloud. Everything went dark outside the windows. For a second, Amy had the feeling she was suffocating. But the black cloud—the ash Dan had just been talking about—disappeared quickly.

The chopper swerved to the right, then veered sharply to the left. It lurched up and down.

"What's going on?" Jake asked.

Another lurch, and Amy felt her stomach drop to her knees.

"Whoa!" Atticus shouted.

"This is better than a roller coaster!" Dan said.

"This isn't good." They were far from Guatemala City now, flying over mountains and jungle that looked like the middle of nowhere. Amy opened the partition dividing the cockpit from the passenger seats and caught the pilot quickly sitting down.

"What's going on?" she asked.

The pilot didn't look at her. "No English."

No English? Hadn't he told her to sit down and buckle

her seat belt? She noticed his coat on the seat next to him. She leaned farther into the cockpit and immediately realized why the pilot had looked like he had a lump under his coat. He had a parachute strapped to his back.

A wave of anxious nausea washed over Amy. "What do you think you're doing?" she demanded. The pilot refused to meet her eye. The chopper lurched again, just missing the side of a mountain.

"He's wearing a parachute!" she told the others. "I think he's going to jump!"

"Pierce must have gotten to him," Dan said.

The pilot jerked on the handle of the cockpit door to his left, trying to open it and throw himself out. "Grab him!" Jake shouted.

Amy ducked out of the way. Jake dove through the partition and grabbed the pilot before he could open the outside door. "Dan, help me!"

Dan reached through the partition door and helped Jake drag the pilot into the passenger area. The chopper immediately began to drop.

"Amy — take the controls!" Jake barked.

Amy crawled over Dan and Jake, who were wrestling the pilot, into the front seat and grabbed the controls. She panicked. Now what?

"Steady this thing!" Jake shouted.

"How?" Amy shrieked back at him.

"I don't know!" Jake called back.

The chopper nosed down toward the trees. She

pulled on the control stick in front of her and the nose tilted up. The chopper didn't rise, but it stopped falling. It leveled and moved forward—straight for the side of a volcano.

"AMY!" Dan screamed.

"I'm trying!" She found a lever on the floor to her left. She hadn't tried that one yet. She yanked on it, praying it would do something good.

The chopper rose. It lifted over the volcano. Amy looked down into the dark abyss at the top and thought she saw a puff of smoke.

The pilot escaped from Jake's hold and threw his upper body into the cockpit, trying to knock her hand away from the controls. "Get him out of here!" she shouted.

Jake, Dan, and Atticus dragged the pilot back to the second row of seats. The chopper dropped fast, down toward a green valley. "Pull up! Up!" Jake shouted.

"I know!" Amy yanked on the lever again with all her might. The chopper rose up toward the sky, pulling out of the valley and almost shaving off the top of a hill. It wobbled. She straightened out and the chopper steadied, but then it started spinning, circling around in the air. Amy frantically tugged at the control stick again, and the chopper nosed forward.

The boys struggled to subdue the pilot, but he wasn't going down without a fight. He managed to unlatch the passenger door. Amy felt the change in pressure. She looked back to see what was happening, and the chopper swerved a deep left. Everyone tumbled over to that side.

"Amy, watch it!" Dan shouted.

Amy concentrated on keeping the chopper steady. The pilot had grabbed Atticus by the arms as a kind of hostage.

"Let him go!" Jake yelled.

Amy didn't dare turn away from the controls — one slip and the chopper would crash, or tip and knock Atticus out. Behind her she heard thumping, grunting, and shouting. But when Jake cried out desperately, "No! No!" she had to turn to see what was happening.

The pilot was leaning out of the helicopter with Atticus clutched in one arm. He was going to jump and take Atticus with him. But the pilot had a parachute, and Atticus didn't.

Dan threw all his weight on one of the pilot's legs, and Jake tugged on his arm, trying to reel him back into the chopper. Suddenly, the pilot screamed.

Amy turned her attention to the front of the chopper. She was about to fly straight into a cliff. She pulled the cyclic up and the chopper rose over the cliff, nearly scraping off its landing skids. Sweat broke out on her forehead. It dripped into her eyes, but she didn't dare release the controls to wipe it away.

"We'll handle this, Amy!" Jake yelled. "Just fly this thing!"

Amy concentrated on the control panel and tried not to look back to see what was happening behind her. But it was hard. The sounds coming from the backseat—grunts, groans of pain, heavy thuds—terrified her. She couldn't see, but she felt each thud like a punch in the stomach.

Dan felt every muscle in his body exert itself, from his straining eyeballs to the toes that curled around the leg of a seat. The pilot hung out the cabin door, bent at the waist, head dangling, still clutching Atticus. Jake was tugging on the pilot's legs and Dan held Att's feet, bracing his legs against a seat. Atticus's eyes were huge with terror as he strained to grab Dan's hand. He was panting, his breath fast and shallow like a terrified rabbit's.

The pilot gave Jake a mighty kick in the chin, knocking him backward. "Ugh!" Jake's grip loosened, and the pilot tumbled out the door.

"Att!" Dan screamed. Atticus's little body seemed to float out into the air over the jungle below. Dan clutched Att's foot, but his sneaker slipped off in his hand. Jake lunged for his brother and caught him by the torso. With a huge effort he heaved his body back into the cabin, Atticus in his arms. They collapsed on the floor.

Dan looked down just before yanking the cabin door shut. The pilot's chute opened as he floated into the jungle and disappeared among the treetops.

CHAPTER 3

The chopper was flying a little steadier now that no one was dangling out the open door, but it swerved left and right. Amy had no idea how to keep it going straight.

"Is everyone all right back there?" she screamed.

Atticus rubbed his legs as if they hurt, but he swallowed and nodded. "I'm okay."

"Amy, can you fly this thing?" Dan asked.

"No!" She scanned the control board in a panic. She knew they were supposed to head north toward Tikal. But which way was north? "Which one of these things is the compass?"

Jake jumped into the copilot's seat. "That's it. I think."

"Maybe we can talk to a control tower or something?" Amy said. "And they could tell me what to do?"

Jake strapped on the pilot's mic and headphones and toyed with the controls until he made radio contact with someone speaking Spanish.

"It's the control tower at Tikal!" said Jake. He fired

off something in Spanish to them. They answered back with something that sounded like a question, and disbelief. Jake replied. Over the radio came shouts of shock and horror.

"What are they saying?" Amy asked Jake.

"They keep asking to speak to the pilot, and when I told them he bailed and a teenage girl was trying to fly to Tikal, they kind of lost it."

"Okay, but what should I DO?"

Jake spoke over the radio in Spanish again. A tidal wave of panicky Spanish flooded back. "Keep your sights about half a mile ahead if you can," Jake translated. He showed her what each of the controls did and how to work the two pedals on the floor. "Head north-northwest, so keep the compass pointed at this number 33." He pointed to the spot where the compass should point.

"What?! How do I do that?"

After another exchange in Spanish, Jake told her how to adjust the cyclic and collective controls and the throttle. She pushed on the cyclic too hard and the chopper started to nosedive.

Dan and Atticus screamed. "Not so hard!" Jake shouted. "Light pressure!"

"Okay, okay!" She could hardly think. Spread out below them was nothing but smoking volcanoes and the thick cover of jungle. No place to land that she could see. And if she couldn't keep this chopper in the air, they'd crash. Their lives were in her hands, and her hands felt about as useful as two bricks.

"Steady," Jake said. "A little more pressure on the right pedal. Now just keep us going like this. . . ."

She pressed too hard on the pedal and the chopper lurched again. *No, stop it, stop it!*

"Whoa!" Dan shouted.

"Ease up! Ease up!" Jake cried.

She snapped her foot off the pedal as if it had suddenly become burning hot, causing another lurch. She tried touching it lightly, and the chopper steadied again. Her heart raced, her hands shook, but she willed herself to focus on the controls. She felt as if she were wrestling with a shark, a big, uncontrollable, dangerous creature; one false move and it could chew you to bits. She glanced at Dan and Atticus in the seats behind her, clutching each other. *I won't let them die*, she told herself. *We won't crash, we won't crash. . . .*

A strong hand gripped her shoulder. She knew without looking that it was Jake's. She didn't say anything, didn't have time to think about it, but it calmed her just a little.

The radio barked Spanish. "The tower's got you on their radar. They'll guide us in," Jake said. "We're almost over the Tikal National Park now. If you can find a clearing, they'll tell you how to land this thing. Head due west."

"A clearing?" Amy scanned the land for an opening in the jungle. She saw nothing but thick vegetation for miles around. But then the trees began to get patchier, as the ruins of temples became visible.

"Lower your altitude to three hundred feet," Jake translated. *"Slowly."*

Amy lowered the collective lever slowly. The front of her forehead throbbed with tension. The three lives in her care—Dan, Jake, Atticus—weighed on her heart so heavily she was afraid it would pull the helicopter down. But the strong hand still gripped her shoulder. That helped.

"Good. Now slow down. Thirty knots. Twenty knots." Amy eyed the speedometer. "Ease the cyclic back and keep your nose up. UP!" Jake added as the nose began to point downward. Amy's heart was in her throat, but she swallowed it down—*Think! Think!*—and pulled the nose up. They were skimming over the tops of the trees. Amy spotted a Mayan pyramid near a strange rectangular clearing—a narrow field of grass stretched between two stone structures. It almost looked like a landing strip, but it wasn't very big.

"I'm going to land there," she told Jake. Biting her lip, she slowed the chopper to a hover over the grass. She pulled the collective lever slowly to lower it. They dropped down even with the tops of the trees, then below the canopy of leaves, until she could practically see each blade of grass. There wasn't much room for error.

The hand on her shoulder did not let go.

The control tower gave more instructions. "Arm the parking brake," Jake translated.

"What does that mean?" Her head was spinning.

Everything was strange—the controls, trying to fly, the orders in Spanish, the jolting pain in her belly. . . .

More Spanish. "I think it's this!" Jake pulled a lever. The chopper's forward momentum stopped and it began to drop fast. They were thirty feet in the air, falling out of the sky straight down to the ground.

"Crash positions!" Amy shouted. Dan and Atticus bent forward in their seats, Atticus covering his eyes. Amy frantically pulled the nose up to slow their descent, but it didn't help. The ground zoomed up into her face. She let go of the controls and covered her head.

Slam! The chopper crashed to the ground, tail smashing against a stone wall. Then the front thudded down. Amy's forehead punched her knee. All was still.

Jake's hand still gripped her shoulder. He'd never let go, not once.

She lifted her head. Jake lifted his. She turned and saw Dan and Atticus crouched on the floor. Atticus raised his head. But Dan didn't move. "Dan! Are you okay?" She reached back and shook him. He sat up, rubbing his temple.

"Is it safe now? Are we on the ground?"

"Yes," Amy said. She tasted metal, and realized her lip was bleeding where she'd been biting it. "Is everybody all right?" She put her hand on Atticus's head, then on Dan's.

Jake nodded at her. "Yes." It was a miracle that no one was hurt.

Amy's door had sprung open on landing. She

unbuckled her seat belt and tumbled out of the chopper. Jake jumped out of his side and helped the younger boys to solid ground. "Dan, you're sure you're okay?" Amy asked. "You too, Att?" They both looked unsteady on their legs.

Atticus straightened up tall, trying to be brave. "Just a few bruises," he squeaked. He couldn't hide the shakiness in his voice.

"I feel like I just got poured out of a blender," Dan said. "But I'm okay."

It was a skill he'd perfected over the years — masking his fear with jokiness — but her bubbling relief made it impossible for her guilt to take hold. "Thank goodness."

"Hey, your mouth's bleeding," Dan said.

"I know." Amy pressed her lips together, tasting the blood again. She inspected the damage. They'd landed on the tail and fallen forward onto the landing skids. The tail rotors had broken off and the tip of the tail was smashed. One of the back passenger windows had shattered and a door hung off its hinges, and their backpacks had been thrown out of the chopper onto the grass. Luckily, the chopper hadn't been too high when they started to crash, or the damage would have been worse.

She took a deep breath and collapsed on the ground. "I'm never doing that again."

"And I never *want* you to do that again," Dan said.

CHAPTER 4

Tikal National Park, Petén, Guatemala

"Where are we?" Atticus asked. They'd landed in the narrow field near a temple. Surrounding the field were rows of steps, sort of like bleachers. Set into one of the walls high overhead was a strange stone hoop covered in glyphs. Dan tried to think of a joke about ancient PE classes, but his brain still felt like it was sloshing in his skull from the crash.

"Wow!" Atticus ran right up to the ring.

"Atticus, how can you care about Mayan ruins at a time like this?" Dan asked wearily. "We just escaped death by a nose hair."

"But this is amazing!" Atticus said.

Dan, Jake, and Amy rested and caught their breath while Atticus ran his hands over the stone glyphs. Dan was glad Att seemed to recover quickly, but he didn't trust this sudden enthusiasm. He knew Atticus was coping in his typical way — by immersing himself in history. Maybe that was why he'd become such a prodigy. His life had had its share of trauma, but he found safety in knowledge, the more obscure, the better.

"Dan, look!" Atticus waved at him. "I've always wanted to see one of these with my own eyes."

When his head stopped spinning, Dan sat up. They seemed to have crashed in some ancient stadium.

"Reminds me a little of a tennis court," Jake said.

"It is," Atticus told them. "It's a *pok-a-tok* court."

"A what?" Dan asked.

"A *pok-a-tok* court," Atticus repeated, as if it were the most obvious thing in the world.

Dan tried to walk, but his legs were wobbly. He let himself plop down on the grass. "I know you're saying something important, Att, but forgive me if I have trouble caring right now."

Sirens blared in the distance, gradually getting closer. "I hope that's an ambulance," Amy said.

Jake shot a piercing glance at her. "Are you hurt?"

"I can't tell. I don't think so, but my arms and legs are numb, and I want you all to be checked out for injuries, too."

The ambulance arrived, followed by a jeep full of Guatemalan soldiers in camouflage uniforms, with green berets on their heads and rifles strapped over their shoulders. "The army?" Dan whispered. "Isn't that overkill?"

"We did crash a helicopter in a national park," Amy reminded him.

Two medics jumped out of the ambulance and checked the kids for injuries. One of them spoke English, and the army captain who oversaw the examinations did, too. "Where is the pilot?" the captain demanded.

"He jumped," Amy explained.

"And he tried to take the little one with him," Dan added, gesturing toward Atticus.

The captain's eyes narrowed in disbelief. "He jumped? Why would he do that?"

"You tell us," Jake said. Dan caught the dirty look Amy flashed him. They knew why the pilot had jumped—he'd taken a bribe from Pierce to let the Cahills die in an "accidental" helicopter crash.

But letting the Guatemalan army in on their troubles wouldn't help. For all they knew, Pierce had an in with them, too. His long arm of evil reached all over the world. "We don't know why he jumped," Amy said. "You can ask him if you can find him out in the jungle."

The captain stared dubiously into the thick forest. Dan knew that it grew so fast it could cover a crashed plane in a matter of days.

The medics finished checking Dan, Amy, Jake, and Atticus for broken bones and signs of concussion. "Some bumps and bruises, but they're okay," one reported to the captain.

"Good. You may go." The captain dismissed the ambulance and crossed his arms over his chest. Dan eyed the pistol in his belt. These guys didn't fool around. "Now, may I ask what you children are doing here in Tikal?"

"We're tourists," Amy said as the ambulance drove away. "We just want to see the ruins, that's all. We have a reservation at the hotel."

As if to confirm Amy's statement, a Tikal park ranger drove up in an SUV. He got out, stared at the crashed helicopter, shook his head, and whistled. "I didn't believe it when the airport called and said you'd landed a helicopter in the *pok-a-tok* court." He shook his head again. "I still don't believe it."

"We're investigating the crash site," the captain told the ranger. "You may take these people to their hotel. We'll be in touch if we need more information."

"All right," Amy said. "You know where we are."

The captain gave her a grim look. "Yes, *señorita*, we do."

The ranger collected the Cahills' bags and loaded them into the SUV. The kids piled into the backseat and let the ranger have the front seat to himself. He started the car, then turned and stared at them as if trying to figure out what kind of strange creatures they might be. "You are alive." It was not a question but an astonished statement. "It is hard to believe."

Dan didn't know how to answer that. Jake said, "Strange but true. And we'd really like to get to the hotel and recover."

But the driver still watched them. "You are the Cahills, yes?" Amy nodded. "*Those* Cahills?"

Obviously, this guy read the tabloids. Dan saw Amy open her mouth wearily as if to answer, but Jake cut her off. "We don't know what you're talking about, dude. Can we get going?"

The driver finally turned toward the steering wheel and put the SUV into drive. "You crash a helicopter on a *pok-a-tok* court, you must expect a few questions."

"What's this *pok-a-tok* everybody's going on about?" Dan asked Atticus in a low voice.

"It was a complicated ball game played by the Maya about four thousand years ago. The goal was to get a ball through this stone hoop without using your hands or feet," Atticus said. "We don't know much about it, other than that."

Dan turned and looked out the back window at the ring receding into the distance. It must have been about twenty feet off the ground. "That seems impossible."

"It was so hard that games went on for days with no score," Atticus said. "Historians think that the losing team was often executed."

"And I thought dodgeball was rough," Dan said.

"Why were they executed?" Amy asked.

"The players might have been prisoners of war," Atticus said. "They were offered as sacrifices to the gods." He looked thoughtful.

"What is it?" Dan asked. When his friend got that look on his face, it meant his brilliant mind was working on something important, like pondering the origins of the universe, or programming a whoopee cushion app.

"Nothing . . . just that the carvings on that stone hoop looked familiar somehow."

The ranger turned down a jungle road, pointing out a tall Mayan pyramid in front of a plaza or town square. Unlike the Egyptian pyramids built of large blocks of cut stone with flat, smooth sides, or the ones in Angkor Wat that looked as if they'd been made of poured wet sand, these were step pyramids, small cut stones forming tall steps that led to the top.

"Can we walk to the top of one of those pyramids?" Dan asked. The sooner they started looking for the crystal, the better.

"Certain ones are open to tourists, yes," the ranger replied. "Tikal was one of the prime centers of Mayan civilization," he told them, "inhabited from the sixth century B.C. to the tenth century A.D. The ancient city has been mapped out. It covered over six square miles and was comprised of over three thousand structures. The whole park area is about two hundred twenty-two square miles. A lot of archaeological treasures are still buried under vegetation." The ranger waved his hand at a dense green grove with a few piles of stone just visible through the brush. "There are thousands of ancient structures buried in this jungle, and we've only excavated a fraction of them." Dan's spirits sank. How were they supposed to find one piece of quartz in all of that?

They drove through lush green jungle. Suddenly, the trees parted and a beautiful ancient city appeared before them. A step pyramid rose two hundred feet at one end, with a long gray staircase up the front. It was surrounded by what looked like houses or palaces around a green village square. "It looks like another planet," Jake said.

"It looks like Yavin," Dan said. "You know, like from *Star Wars*?"

"That's right," the ranger told them. "George Lucas filmed scenes from the first Star Wars movie here in 1977." He drove on. In the distance, the gray stone tops of other ancient temples poked up through the green, and beautiful exotic birds chattered in the treetops. Dan spotted a funny-looking animal with raccoon eyes and a long, ringed tail scampering down a jungle path.

"A coati!" Atticus said.

"Very good, little boy," the ranger said to Atticus's obvious annoyance. "You'll see coatis all over the place here."

They passed a very tall tree — maybe one hundred feet tall — with large thorns covering the trunk. The upper branches spread over the road like a canopy. "A *ceiba*," the ranger told them. "Sacred tree of the Maya. They believed its roots reached into the underworld and its branches held up the sky. The souls of the dead climbed its branches to get to the heavens."

A truck passed by with four men riding in the back, axes and shovels over their shoulders. The ranger frowned. "Tikal is also an important rain forest reserve for protected plants, birds, and animals." He glanced at the truck as it disappeared in his rearview mirror. "We patrol the area as well as we can, but unfortunately a few poachers manage to slip in from time to time."

"Poachers? What do they steal?" Amy asked.

"They hunt crocodiles, pumas, and jaguars for their skins, harvest endangered flowers, or chop down rare trees for the valuable wood," the ranger replied. "Sometimes we find secret poacher logging camps deep in the forest. They're almost impossible to spot under the cover of the jungle."

"Have you ever heard of a riven rock, or riven crystal, being found in one of these temples?" Amy asked.

"Or shocked quartz?" Jake added.

The ranger shook his head. "The temples are made of local limestone. Not much quartz is found in this area, unless the Maya traded for it."

They spent the rest of the drive in silence.

They checked into their hotel and headed for their rooms. Amy opened her backpack to make sure the serum flask had survived the crash. She held the flask to the light. The poison-green fluid—undiluted, full-strength—was as deadly as it looked. It imparted awesome power to the person who drank it—for a week. And then it killed them. She shuddered and put the vial back inside her pack.

She took a shower and changed, then went next

door to meet the others in Dan and Atticus's room. Jake was there, hanging out with the other boys. Dan was losing to Atticus at chess. The TV was on, tuned to an international news channel. Dan's T-shirt was smudged from the bumpy trip, a big footprint stamped on the front.

"What's that footprint on your shirt?" Amy asked.

Dan glanced down at it. "Must have been from that dirtbag pilot, when I was holding his leg trying to keep him from bailing on us."

Amy sighed. "Aren't you going to take a shower? Or at least change?"

"Why? Are we meeting with the queen of England or something?" Dan asked.

"Speaking of the queen . . ." Jake turned up the volume on the TV. The footage showed a handsome man shaking hands with Queen Elizabeth, his airbrushed blond wife curtsying beside him.

"American media mogul J. Rutherford Pierce met with Queen Elizabeth at a reception yesterday on the last leg of his European tour," the news announcer reported. "Pierce has been meeting with world leaders in a clear indication that he's preparing to run for political office. Pundits are expecting him to throw his hat into the ring in the race for US president very soon."

"President Pierce," Dan said. "I don't like the sound of that."

"It does have a sinister ring to it," Amy agreed.

"The way Pierce operates, it's a short step from president to dictator," Dan said.

Amy watched Pierce's wife, Debi Ann, who hovered in the background. The contrast between her and her husband was striking. She looked dull and bleached out next to her vibrant, glowing husband, almost like a different species of human.

Because he's taking the serum, Amy realized. *And Debi Ann isn't.*

Pierce took a modified version of the serum, a very weak, diluted dose. Enough to enhance his power, but not enough to kill him. "What do we know about his wife?" she asked Jake.

"Not much. Wait—they're cutting to an interview with the two of them now."

The news showed a clip from an interview taped in the Pierces' elegant home in Boston. Debi Ann sat beside Pierce on a blue silk sofa, smiling and nodding mechanically. "What about you, Debi Ann?" the interviewer asked. "I read that you grew up in a family of scientists. What was that like?"

Debi Ann nodded. "We had a chemistry lab in the basement." She smiled at the memory. "That was our playroom. We Starlings were all talented scientists."

Dan and Amy jumped at the same time. "Starling?" Amy gasped. "Did she say *Starling*?"

"Did you see the look on Pierce's face when she mentioned it?" Dan said. "He was furious!"

Amy had noticed a flash of anger cross Pierce's

serenely tanned face at the mention of the name Starling. Although it'd mean nothing to 99 percent of the audience, he clearly didn't want Debi Ann to mention that very important fact. The Starlings were related to Amy and Dan. If Debi Ann was a *Starling*, it could only mean one thing. She was a Cahill, too.

"She's Pierce's link to the serum!" Dan exclaimed.

"He must know all about the family, the branches, and everything, through his wife," Jake said.

"But I researched her," Amy protested. "Both her and Pierce, relentlessly. I scoured the Internet and no Cahill connection ever came up. How could that be?"

"Ask Pony," Dan said. He dialed Attleboro, putting his phone on speaker.

A smooth British voice answered. "Dan? You made it to Tikal, I see."

"Yes," Amy cut in. "We all made it. Just barely."

"Amy, so glad you're all right," Ian purred. "Everyone else present and accounted for? Dan? Atticus? That other one . . . what's his name? Joke?"

Amy turned red, her eyes involuntarily cutting over to Jake, who scowled. "That's beneath you, Ian," Amy said. "Listen, we need you to put Pony on a deep search for information about Debi Ann Pierce. Try searching for Deborah Starling as well."

"I'm on it." More purring. This time it wasn't coming from Ian but from an actual cat. "Ugh, get away from me, you filthy feline!" Ian grumbled.

"Hi, Saladin!" Dan called out.

"Meow!" the Egyptian Mau replied.

"Are Ian and Hamilton feeding you well?" Amy asked. "Ian, is Saladin getting enough red snapper?"

"We're not pet-sitting here, you know," Ian grumbled. "We're actually busy helping you save the world, in case you've forgotten."

"And we appreciate it," Amy said. There was a knock on the door. "We have to go. Tell Pony to get on the Debi Ann thing stat."

Jake opened the door to a tall, dark woman in a safari skirt suit.

"Hello," she said. "I'm Dr. Casanova. An Amy Cahill arranged to meet with me?"

"Come in." Jake stepped aside to let her through. "We've been expecting you."

"Thank you." She nodded, glanced around the room, and sat down in the one chair that didn't have boys' clothes strewn over it. "I'm not usually available for private consultations, but when El Presidente asks for a favor . . ." Amy had pulled some Cahill strings to get a private meeting with Guatemala's leading expert on Tikal, hoping to make quick work of locating the riven crystal. "I understand you have some questions about one of the temples here?"

"Yes — only we don't know which temple," Amy said. "We're looking for something called a 'riven crystal,' or shocked quartz." She showed the archaeologist a photo of shocked quartz, taken through a microscope. The stone had waves of rainbow-colored layers striated by sharp black lines that looked almost like lightning bolts. It was strange and beautiful.

Dr. Casanova nodded. "That's not native to this area, but it is found in the Yucatán. The people of Tikal traded with the Yucatán and could easily have gotten some of this crystal. I've never seen it here, however."

"The stone only looks this way under a microscope," Atticus explained. "It would be hard to spot it among other stones, since it looks like ordinary quartz to the naked eye."

Dr. Casanova eyed the eleven-year-old Atticus warily. He was so smart and mature for his age that some adults found him threatening, as if they were afraid of being shown up by a kid. Amy hoped Dr. Casanova was not that kind of adult.

"Nevertheless," the archaeologist said. "The temples that have been excavated have all been thoroughly examined. A piece of quartz, shocked or not, would have been noticed in all the limestone."

"But there could be a piece of shocked quartz in one of the unexcavated temples, right?" Amy said.

"Anything is possible," Dr. Casanova conceded. "Even landing a helicopter on a *pok-a-tok* court, from what I hear."

Dan started to laugh, but it died in his throat when he saw the stern look on the archaeologist's face. "Yeah, sorry about that. It was an emergency landing."

"You might have crashed into priceless

archaeological treasures," Dr. Casanova said. "You could have ruined them forever."

"Uh, yeah. We also could have died," Dan pointed out.

"That's not my concern," Dr. Casanova sniffed.

Amy caught Dan exchanging an *oh, brother* look with Atticus.

"I know *pok-a-tok* is something of a mystery to us," Atticus said. "But have you learned anything new about it?" Amy wasn't sure whether he was changing the subject to be diplomatic, or it was just natural curiosity spilling out. Either way, she was grateful.

"We know it was very important—like baseball and football are to you," Dr. Casanova replied, her face softening slightly. "There are relics depicting men playing *pok-a-tok* all over the Mayan world. You'll see it as you explore the park—*the parts that are open to the public*, that is."

Amy cleared her throat. "I believe we have permission to explore the unexcavated ruins as well." She took an official-looking piece of paper from her bag and showed it to Dr. Casanova. The same strings she'd pulled to get a private meeting with the archaeologist had also convinced the government to pressure park officials to break the rules for them. Or at least, that was what the paper said. In fact, she'd gotten Pony to rig up some phony forms that looked very real.

The archaeologist frowned. "I can provide a guide to make sure you do nothing to harm the artifacts."

Amy suppressed a grimace. A guide was the last thing they wanted. They didn't want to harm anything, but if they found the riven crystal, they were going to take a sample of it. She felt a little guilty about desecrating ancient ruins, but it had to be weighed against the greater good. Without that crystal there would be no serum antidote, and without the antidote . . . well, it would be Pierce's world, literally. They'd all just be living in it, Dr. Casanova included.

"In any case, it would take years — decades — to search the entire lost city of Tikal for one stone," Dr. Casanova said, getting up to leave. "It hardly seems worth the effort."

"It is to us," Dan said.

"Why?"

"School science project," Dan lied smoothly, just as he'd been doing for years. Lying to security guards, librarians, Interpol agents — anyone who stood between the Cahills and their mission.

Dr. Casanova looked skeptical but apparently decided not to pursue it any further. This was one of those times when being "just kids" was helpful. "If you have any more questions, feel free to call my office. Good-bye." She left.

"We don't have years to find that crystal," Amy said. "We need it now! There must be a way to find it quickly. Something in the book. Some clue . . ."

Their eyes all turned to the book. It contained all the answers they needed, if only they could decode them.

CHAPTER 5

They left their rooms and went to eat in the hotel restaurant. Everyone ordered *pepian de pollo*, a rich, spicy, dark red chicken stew, sprinkled with roasted squash and sesame seeds and served with rice and corn tortillas.

"Have to try the national dish while we're here," Jake said, sounding more like someone's goofy dad than a shaggy-haired hipster. Although Dan hated to think about his sister's boyfriends, he had to admit Jake would've been a good fit—one ubernerd deserved another. Or at least, they would've been a good fit until Amy decided to shut down and cut ties with everyone who cared about her.

"I'm learning a lot about myself on this trip," Dan said, matching Jake's cheerful tone. "For example, if it comes with tortillas, I like it."

"What about you, Att?" Jake asked. "Do you like the *pepian*?"

Atticus took a bite of stew and nodded. "Delicious."

That's not like him, Dan thought. He and Atticus

usually lived as if life were one big eating contest. But Atticus seemed distracted. He stared at everything, from the pictures on the restaurant walls to the menu, as if they might hold the keys to the universe. After lunch, he barely nodded when Dan asked if he wanted to go for a walk.

"The answer is right in front of our eyes," he told Dan. "I know it is. If I can just *see* it . . ."

They stopped in the museum gift shop. "There's not much here," Dan said. "Just a bunch of dishes and woven fabrics—"

Atticus was staring at a large platter decorated with glyphs. Dan saw a scowling face with a large nose, a glyph that could have been a bird or a hand with the thumb up, and others that just looked like squiggles. Atticus took a small notebook and pen from his pocket and began copying the images on the plate.

"What?" Dan asked.

"That's it. . . ." Atticus shook his head. "Come on!"

He ran back to the hotel, his shorter legs moving so quickly, Dan had trouble keeping up. When they reached their room, Atticus burst inside and opened Olivia's book, flipping carefully through until he got to the page he'd been staring at on the chopper, the one with strange glyphs that he hadn't been able to make sense of. Between each glyph were two letters and a number, such as NE224, SW305, and so on. He pointed to a square containing a foot and a circle, and another that looked like the face of a monster.

"I didn't know if Olivia had copied these figures from somewhere, or if she'd made them up, or if they were just doodles," Atticus said. "Now I'm sure she copied them from the Maya." He studied the page intently, and then began scribbling in his notebook.

"Atticus, what is it?" Dan demanded. He stared at the page, trying to make sense of the figures on it. It didn't look like a language. They were almost like drawings, but very abstract. If they were drawings, Dan didn't get what was happening in them.

"The glyphs," Atticus said.

"What about them?"

Atticus kept scribbling. "I'll tell you if I'm right — but I'm pretty sure I am."

Dan went to get Amy and Jake, brooding alone in their rooms. "Atticus is onto something. He thinks."

By the time they all gathered back in Dan and Atticus's room, Atticus had stopped writing. "I've got it," he announced. "The glyphs in the Codex are based on the game. *Pok-a-tok!*"

"What do you mean?" Jake asked.

"The symbols in Olivia's book refer to different aspects of the game." Atticus opened his laptop and searched for a painting showing Mayan *pok-a-tok* players. They wore large, fancy headdresses made of feathers, bracelets and earrings, skirts or kilts, and in front of them bounced a large black ball. Then Att showed them the glyphs in the book, which looked mostly like squiggles to Dan. But if he tried hard enough, he could see a man in a headdress bouncing a ball off his shoulder in one image, a ball going through a stone hoop in another, and so on. "In actuality, they form a code. If I follow the symbols almost as if I were following a ball game—first this player hits the ball to that player, who knocks it to that part of the field, etcetera—the code forms a map." He had drawn a graph on a piece of tissue paper and plotted dots along the graph. Each dot represented a ball player. "The numbers and letters between each glyph tell me the distance between each player, and which direction they're standing in. For instance—" He pointed to a glyph of a player in a headdress, next to the number N873. "This man is passing the ball to the next player, who is standing 873 feet to the north of him. Of course, in a real game the players would never stand that far apart. The court isn't anywhere near that big. But these glyphs don't depict a real game. They're a code." Atticus shook his head. "It took me forever to figure out what those numbers were supposed to mean."

He'd printed out a satellite map of the entire Tikal park, showing every hill, every ruin, excavated or not. "When I lay this paper over a map of Tikal—" He set the paper over the map. Many of the dots Atticus had drawn corresponded to temples, pyramids, and other ruined landmarks on the satellite picture.

"It works!" Dan cried.

But Atticus frowned. "Wait—there's nothing on the satellite to correspond with this dot." He pointed to a "player" on his map that seemed to be sitting in the middle of the jungle. "Or this one, either."

Jake leaned over the map, tracing a line from one dot to the next. "We need those landmarks to get us through the jungle without getting lost."

Amy pored over the map. "Wait a second—maybe there are ruins there. We just can't see them on this satellite map. Most of them haven't been excavated yet."

"I think I see something whitish gray there." Dan used the magnifying glass app on his phone to look more closely at the picture. "See? There is a temple or something there. It's just mostly covered in vegetation."

Amy pointed to the final dot on the map, a spot deep in the jungle, the site of some unexcavated ruins believed to be a second-century temple. "That must be where the crystal is," she said. "Atticus, you're a genius!" She gave him a congratulatory fist bump.

"We already knew that," Jake said proudly.

Dan looked out the window. "It's getting dark out."

"And it's late," Amy said. "We don't want to get lost in the jungle tonight. We'll leave at dawn."

CHAPTER 6

Trilon Laboratories
Delaware

Nellie Gomez sat in her small office, pretending to read research reports on the genetic effects of radiation on rats. She was waiting for her coworkers—that is, her employees, sort of, since she was the manager of this particular department—to leave. *Go home already, drones!* she thought. She stared at the last two research chemists left in the lab—Gerry Wentworth and Brent Beckelheimer—willing them with her brainpower to leave. It wasn't working.

So much for my psychic abilities, she thought, hiding a copy of *Punk Rock Confidential* behind *The Journal of Genetic Research*. It still shocked her when she woke up in the morning to realize she'd be spending her day as the head of a sterile lab in a corporate pharmaceutical complex in Delaware. She wasn't quite sure how she—a punk-rocker-slash-aspiring-chef from Boston—became Dr. Nadine Gormey, the boss of a bunch of brainy chemists with PhDs from Hopkins and MIT, but it was lucky that she was. Because something dangerous and very secret was happening in this lab, and the fate of the world depended on her stopping it.

Beckelheimer stuck his head into Nellie's office. "Uh, excuse me, Dr. Gormey, I guess Dr. Wentworth and I will be going now."

"All right, Dr. Beckelheimer. I suppose you can't work twenty-four hours a day. You're only human after all, right? Of course, I'll be staying late as usual." Nellie waved the scientific journal she was pretending to read at him, just catching the music magazine before it slipped out and revealed how seriously she was goofing off. "Got to burn the midnight oil again tonight. See you in the morning."

"Good night, Dr. Gormey." The two scientists finally left. Now Nellie could start her real work: snooping.

She waited awhile, listening to the sounds of the building, waiting for that level of absolute quiet that meant everyone had gone. Then she crept through the dark hallways, lit now only by emergency lights, and up to the fourth floor, until she came to a vending machine. She took a special "A" ID she'd stolen from a sales rep, a more trusted worker (and rightly so, she thought with a snicker), from a chain hooked to her pants pocket and slipped it into the machine. The machine opened like a door. In fact, it *was* a door—a secret door that led to the basement labs where the serious research was being done. If the regular work of

Trilon Labs was top secret, the basement lab work was on the level of *If I told you, I'd have to kill you.*

The door slid shut behind her as she descended the stairs, keeping an eye out for the heavily armed guards who could be lurking around every corner. She was looking for Sammy Mourad.

Sammy was a brilliant young grad student, a Cahill cousin of Dan and Amy's, with a genius for biochemistry. He'd been working at Columbia University when Dan asked him to make a sample of the Cahill serum for him. The formula had gotten into the wrongest of wrong hands—Pierce's hands, to be specific. And of course, Pierce wasn't about to let such a useful researcher get away so easily.

Nellie had stumbled upon these secret basement labs and found Sammy working there. He was being held prisoner, but he refused to be rescued.

"Don't you see," he'd told Nellie. "I'm in the perfect position to stop him. You and I both are. We're inside."

"I know that," Nellie had said. "But he's holding you captive. . . ."

"Believe me, I'd love to get out of here," Sammy had said. "But I can sabotage his work from the inside, or try to, at least."

Nellie sighed a funny kind of shivery, happy/sad sigh. He was so brave, risking his life for the good of the world, and for her kiddos, too. Courage plus dark good looks and nerdy charm—that made for irresistible Nellie-bait. Of course, Nellie was risking her life, too, but she was used to that.

They hadn't figured out a secure way to communicate yet, so Nellie sneaked downstairs to check on him every chance she got. The basement was a white labyrinth, hallways branching off hallways and circling back on themselves in a way that seemed deliberately confusing. Crouching under windows, flattening herself against walls to avoid cameras, Nellie made her way through the maze to Sammy's lab. She took a left through an unfamiliar door and wandered past a row of one-way windows. She peeked carefully inside and saw lab after lab, each more sophisticated than the last, with one or two white-coated scientists working doggedly around the clock, blind to anything happening outside the tiny world of the lab they were locked in.

She paused outside the lab where she'd last seen Sammy and peered through the window. A shade had been drawn over it, but she could just barely see through a crack left open at the bottom. . . .

The lab was empty. Lights out. Sammy wasn't there. And it looked like nobody was working in that lab at the moment.

She panicked. A shot of adrenaline burst through her bloodstream and raised her pulse. Where was he? Was he all right?

Nellie heard footsteps — heavy, booted footsteps — coming in her direction. Frantically, she tried a door. It was locked. She tried another. They were all locked. She spotted a swinging door at the end of the corridor and pushed through it. She waited, holding her breath, until the footsteps stomped by, fading as they went down the corridor.

She looked around. She seemed to be in a men's room. *Better get out of here,* she thought. Then she noticed another door beyond the last toilet stall. Probably just a janitor's closet. But if a soda machine could lead to a secret basement, who knew what lay behind a janitor's closet door?

She tried the knob and, miraculously, it opened. It was a closet, holding a rolling bucket and a mop. But the mop, she noticed, was dry and bleach white. It hadn't been used. Maybe it was new. Or maybe it was a decoy.

She pressed against the back wall of the closet. It didn't move.

Okay, so maybe it was just a janitor's closet after all.

Dr. Nadine Gormey doesn't give up that easily.

She lifted the mop and put it down. She rolled the bucket out of the closet. Nothing. She picked up a dust pan and a brush, then tried brushing the back of the wall. She said, "Open Sesame!" It was a long shot, but you never knew what might work.

In this case, however, nothing worked.

She took a moment to look around the men's room. It wasn't as if she'd never been in a men's room before—the bathroom line at the Rat in Boston got so long that girls took over the men's room all the time, shouting, "Revolution!" in true punk-rock fashion. And this one didn't hold anything unusual that she could see. Toilet stalls. Urinals. Sinks. Soap. Paper towel dispensers *and* hand dryers. Nice that they gave the guys a choice.

She pressed on the soap dispensers, pulled out paper towels, pressed on the hand dryer. Nothing but soap and hot air.

Back to the closet. She stared into it as if it were a mysterious cave holding a secret. Something was not right about that closet.

Then she noticed a hook with a broom hanging from it. Some instinct, honed after two years of wild adventures with Amy and Dan, told her to tug on the hook. Sure enough, the back wall of the closet slid open to reveal yet another hallway.

Nellie stepped over the bucket into this new, even more secret area. Trilon Labs had more layers than an Indonesian thousand-layer cake. All in the service of hiding stuff.

The place had a lot of secrets.

At the end of the short corridor was a windowed door. She walked toward it and peered through the window.

There he was. All alone, dropping a chemical onto a slide and peering at it through a microscope, his handsome features stern and serious with work. Sammy.

The door was locked. Nellie tapped on the window. Sammy looked over. He lit up, his face transformed by happy surprise.

Open the door, dummy! Nellie thought. He ran to the

door and opened it, pulling her inside.

"I was hoping you would find me," Sammy said. "Sometimes even the guards can't find me here. They forget to bring my meals."

"Are you okay?" Nellie asked.

"I'm okay. Any news from the outside world?"

"Amy and Dan are in Guatemala—one step closer to making the antidote, I hope."

"When they find it, we're going to need it," Sammy said. "I just got crystal clear orders to speed things up. Pierce wants a safe, mass-produced serum ready to go in the next week."

"Before he announces his candidacy." Nellie shuddered at the thought of all those Patriotist idiots in their tricorne hats . . . enhanced and superpowerful. Ruling the world.

"And the people who are against him . . ." She didn't have to finish the sentence. It would be impossible to oppose him. He would have absolute power.

"Yeah." Sammy nodded sadly. "I've been working as slowly as I can. I've managed to bluff and stall so far, but I don't know how much longer I can keep it up. If I don't come up with some results soon . . ." Sammy swallowed. "I'm trying to find a way to sabotage the research without anyone noticing right away," Sammy explained. "But it's tricky. I want you safely out of here before they figure out what we're up to."

"Don't worry about me," Nellie said. "Just stop Pierce."

There was a noise outside the room. "Someone's coming!" Sammy whispered. "Get out of here, quick!"

Nellie ran to the door. She peered through the window and heard the sound of boots in the corridor. "Too late! I've got to hide somewhere in here."

Sammy set a rack of lab coats near the door. "When they open the door, hide behind it, using the coats for cover."

"This is the first place they'll look!"

"Shhh!" The footsteps stopped just outside the door. There was a sound of keys rattling.

Nellie threw herself against the wall and wriggled behind the coats as the key turned in the lock and the door flung open. A guard dressed in a dark khaki combat uniform and armed with a machine gun stepped into the lab. "Everything okay in here?"

"Everything's fine," Sammy said. "But, oh, do you think I could get more nacho chips with my lunch tomorrow? And maybe a spicier flavor, like Mexican Fiesta?"

The guard grunted. "I'm not in charge of your lunch."

"Oh. Sorry. I just thought maybe you could convey the message to the kitchen, or wherever the slop you feed me comes from. It gets pretty boring down here all by myself, and food's just about the only thing I have to look forward to."

He likes food, she thought. She was holding her breath and praying that this huge, muscular, armed guard wouldn't catch her, but that didn't stop her from melting a little over Sammy. *He doesn't just like it, he's particular about it. Like me. Maybe someday, if we ever get out of this mess, I'll cook a meal for him that will make his taste buds fall in love.*

"Look," the guard said. "I don't want to know anything about your food or how bored you are. I'm just supposed to make sure everything's okay, and to see if you made any progress today."

"Progress? Hmm, let's see. . . ." Through the screen of coats Nellie could see Sammy pick up his microscope and move it to a table facing the back wall of the lab, away from the door. *Good thinking, Mourad,* she thought. If he could distract the guard for long enough, maybe she could slip through the door.

Sammy peered into the scope. "Oh, my gosh!"

"What? What is it?" The guard hurried over to him.

"I've just made the most amazing discovery!" Sammy cried.

That's my cue. Nellie slipped out of the room, leaving the door ajar so it wouldn't be heard. She crept down the short corridor and through the false wall of the janitor's closet. As she was closing the wall-door behind her, she heard Sammy say, "Whoops. Sorry. False alarm."

Sammy was her kind of guy. They'd find a way to stop Pierce, between the two of them. But it had to be soon, before Pierce realized Sammy was not cooperating — and made him pay.

CHAPTER 7

Attleboro, Massachusetts

"Come to me, Debi baby. . . ." Pony used his mouse like a pistol, his fingers flying over the keyboard of his trusty Ponyrific computer. He'd named it Ponyrific because he'd made it himself, from the best parts of the best machines out there, to suit his special needs.

He paused to reach for a slice of pizza, which he demolished in two huge bites. Pony was a skinny, perpetually starving hacker in black glasses, an old pro at nineteen. He wore his long hair pulled back in a ponytail, away from his face. His "mournful hound-dog face," as Nellie had once called it. He smiled, thinking of Nellie. She was one crazy-cool chick.

He'd been given a lot of tough assignments since signing on to work for the Cahill kids, but this was a new one. Amy had asked him to find a link between Debi Ann Pierce and a Deborah Starling, or any Cahill connection at all. Amy was convinced they were one and the same person, and Pony trusted Amy. She was one sharp kid. He would have thought it was amazing that she was only sixteen, if he didn't know so many computer prodigies who were the same age.

Normally, this assignment would be a piece of cake for a digital cowboy—his preferred term—like Pony. Beneath him, even. But as he scoured the Internet, looked behind every mention of Debi Ann Pierce, he was beginning to get discouraged. He was coming up with nothing. There was a lot of stuff about Debi Ann, mostly puff piece magazine interviews about her favorite recipes and her vast collection of teddy bears. In places where it would seem obvious to ask her about her family background, there was a strange silence.

And then it dawned on him. Someone had done a scrub. A very thorough scrub.

His Pony Sense started tingling. Anything that could be used to connect Debi Ann and the Cahills had been deleted. Completely.

That was almost impossible to do. The Internet was a vast sea of words and images, uncontrollable, full of hidden corners of the past.

That was the conventional wisdom, anyway. You weren't supposed to be able to scrub the Internet.

A scrub meant someone was hiding something big. It meant there was a juicy bit of info out there somewhere to be rustled up. And he was just the cowboy to rustle it. Yippie-yi-yi-ay.

Pony cracked his knuckles, tipped the brim of an imaginary cowboy hat at an imaginary pretty schoolmarm, muttered, "Evenin', ma'am," to the imaginary schoolmarm, and went to work.

Now that he'd figured out what had happened to any hint of a link between Debi Ann and the Cahills, Pony was pretty sure he could find a way around it.

With one hand he felt around the pizza box for more sustenance. Nothing but cardboard. The pizza was gone. He frowned and went back to work. Here he was working in the ritziest digs he'd ever seen — the command center on the Cahill estate — where they had everything a hacker could want: a private satellite, top-of-the-line equipment, custom security, and airtight firewalls . . . everything. But they couldn't seem to get enough pizza to feed the crew.

Pony had his own private corner in the command center, across the vast room from where the Cahill dudes did their thing. It was a strange new experience for Pony, working with other people, being part of a team. That wasn't the Hacker Way, and it took some getting used to. Ian Kabra, the slinky Brit, wasn't the friendliest guy Pony had ever met but he was a quick thinker, good at coming up with sneaky strategies. Pony gave Hamilton Holt a wide berth — Ham was a big dude and quick to throw a punch, which Pony was eager to avoid. But he had to admit Ham had a nose for security and was even a decent hacker in his own right. Pony liked Jonah Wizard the best. Jonah was laid-back but smart, and he understood that Pony wasn't just a computer scientist — he was an artist. It took a highly refined sense of rhythm and finesse to surf the web the way Pony did. He'd been a hip-hop fan forever, and Jonah was one of his favorite rappers. Too bad the guy was on hiatus. But now that Pony was inside the Cahill compound, he understood why Jonah wanted to drop out of the limelight. For this family, the limelight was nothing but trouble.

Pony did a search of the Starling family until he found an old photo on a genealogy site. It was labeled THE STARLING FAMILY, 1975, and it showed fifteen people, adults and kids of all ages, who looked as if they'd gathered for a birthday or some other big occasion. But, weirdly, Pony noticed as he looked closer, they were all in costume. A boy tagged FRANK STARLING wore a white fright wig, glasses, and a big white mustache à la Albert Einstein. There was a woman, Candice Jones Starling, dressed as Marie Curie, with green paint on her hands — to indicate radiation poisoning, Pony assumed. She held a beaker in her hand. A gray-haired man tagged as Eustace Starling posed on an old-fashioned tricycle with a huge front wheel, dressed as Thomas Edison. They were all, every last member of the family, dressed up as famous scientists, and each one was tagged with a name . . . except for one little girl, about five years old, holding binoculars to her eyes while a toy chimp rested at her feet. Her costume, Pony guessed, was young Jane Goodall. She was the only one without a Starling name attached to her. Maybe she was a neighbor's kid, not part of the family, but that

was unlikely, since she was dressed up in costume like the others. Pony had a hunch.

There was only one other person — besides the digital cowboy himself — with the skillz to pull off this kind of hacking operation. April May.

Pony hacked into Boston City Hall files to check on Debi Ann's maiden name. There it was in black and white: Debi Ann Stapleton. But when he looked into that, he found that the name had been "corrected" recently. *By Her Supreme Highness, no doubt.*

He sat back to admire her work. She was a genius, and she was thorough. She let nothing get past her. That was why Pony was suspicious that she'd let him follow her trail this way. What was she up to? Was she trying to tell him something?

Or was she trying to lead him astray?

Jonah Wizard passed through the command center, looking for something to eat. "Yo, man, you ate all the pizza?"

Pony shrugged. "I've been working ten hours straight. I need something to keep me going."

"Looks like I gotta eat sushi again." Jonah left in a huff. "Keep at it, whatever you're doing." Jonah gave Pony's hand a casual slap as he walked away. Pony tried to act cool about it, but whoa—Jonah Wizard just gave him five. Like it was no big thing.

Teamwork had its upsides. Sometimes.

It's a new world, P-Man, he said to himself. He gave another tip of his imaginary cowboy hat and went back to work.

CHAPTER 8

Tikal, Guatemala

"Atticus, how much farther?" Dan slapped another mosquito on his arm, then wiped the sweat from his forehead. It was only nine o'clock in the morning, but the sun was already burning the back of his neck as he slogged through the humid jungle air.

Amy, Dan, Jake, and Atticus had set out at dawn in search of the temple that held the riven crystal, following the map Atticus had drawn by connecting the dots in Olivia's book. Two and a half hours later and there was still no sign of the temple.

"From what I can tell of the distances on this map, we're almost there," Atticus said. "Another half hour or so, maybe."

Dan groaned. It had been exciting to hike through the jungle at dawn, seeing howler monkeys, exotic birds, strange plants, and huge colorful flowers, hearing the distant roar of pumas and jaguars. But now that the sun was higher in the sky, the heat was punishing. His hair was damp under his Red Sox cap, and his skin was like candy to the mosquitos. The jungle was deep green and stretched for miles in all directions, as far as Dan could see. He tried to imagine what it had been like to live in this place thousands of years ago, when it was a thriving city. They passed a sign that said, GROUP F. Beyond it was a large plaza and a stone pyramid.

"That's Temple III," Atticus told him. "It was the last structure built here, in A.D. 869, and archaeologists think that the last ruler of Tikal, Chi'taam, might be buried there. But if he is, they haven't found his tomb yet. By the time he died, this city was on the decline and would soon be abandoned."

"What happened?" Dan asked.

"No one's really sure," Atticus replied. "But it's likely that the city was overpopulated, and there was a drought, which brought on water shortages and famine. Thousands died and the civilization never recovered."

They crossed through the grassy plaza, a shortcut to the next trail.

"This was once a marketplace. Farmers sold their produce here, and during Tikal's heyday, traders from all over the Mayan world came to sell their goods. Maybe the riven crystal we're looking for was sold to a priest right here in this marketplace."

Dan tried to entertain himself on the long hike by imagining the priests in their temples, wearing fierce animal masks to please the gods, and warlike Mayan kings ruling from their palaces, heavy feathered head-dresses weighing on their heads. They didn't have time to study the ruins closely, but every time they passed a set of ancient stairs, the crumbling wall of a town square, or a tunnel leading to rooms where people lived thousands of years ago, he got a chill. And in this heat, chills of any kind were welcome.

The clayey mud sucked at his feet. There were a lot of ruins in this jungle. A *lot*. And when you're hot, sweaty, and tired, after a while the ruins all start blurring together into one big, stony mess.

"Atticus, are you sure you picked out the right temple?" Amy asked. Normally, her questioning Att would have bugged Dan, but he caught the same uncertainty on Att's face that she must have seen.

"I'm pretty sure," Atticus admitted. "But there was one key glyph in the book I couldn't decipher. Unless I misunderstood it, it didn't fit with the *pok-a-tok* theme. I was hoping we could get by without it. . . ."

"Which one? Show it to me," Amy said.

She and Atticus were leading the group, following the map to the letter, being very careful to mark their way. Getting lost in this dense jungle would be a disaster. They traveled light and fast, carrying only their backpacks, Olivia's book, and some water. Dan wished they'd also brought a couple of gallons of soda.

The trail they hiked was nothing more than a narrow dirt path, overgrown with ferns and vines that they had to hack out of the way. Up ahead was the stone entrance to some kind of ancient house. It had only been partially excavated, but it looked cool and dark inside.

"We'll stop there and rest for a minute," Amy said.

"You're going to let us rest? That's kind of you," Dan snapped.

Amy's eyes flashed at him angrily. "We've got to get the crystal and get back before dark, Dan. You know that."

"I know," he said, pushing aside his guilt. They sat down to rest in the shade of the stone entrance.

"Look, we're almost there. You'll feel better after you've had a little water and something to eat."

After their rest they continued through the jungle, which grew hotter and more humid every minute. About half an hour later, Atticus stopped in front of a mass of vines and branches. "This is it."

"*This* is it?" Dan asked. It looked like a hill. There was no sign of any ancient ruins. Just a lot of tangled-up vines. "Are you sure?"

Att glanced down at the map and nodded. "I'm pretty sure." He ripped away some vines until a wooden stela, or threshold, appeared. Jake stepped in to help him clear the doorway. The stela was carved with glyphs Dan couldn't decipher, but one image was clear: the face of a laughing monkey.

"That's it," Atticus said. "There was a monkey mask right next to the *pok-a-tok* code. There was still the other glyph I never figured out, but this is a good sign."

"Thank goodness," Amy said. Dan could hear the relief in her voice. "Let's get that crystal."

Jake cleared out the entrance and they crawled into the ruined temple. The ceiling had caved in at some point, so once they crawled through a tunnel-like entrance, they found themselves surrounded by four crumbling walls under open sky.

"What are we looking for, Atticus?" Dan asked.

"Any structure that could be an altar, and a piece of stone that looks different from the limestone around it," Atticus said.

They each took one wall, clearing away jungle growth until they could see stone. It was hot, hard work, and they had to be careful not to destroy anything. Someday this ruin would be excavated and might hold valuable secrets of the past. But for now it held a key ingredient to the serum antidote.

"I think I found an altar!" Jake called out at last.

They all hurried over to look. Atticus ran his hands carefully over the stone. Screaming animal faces were carved into the rock, each one representing a Mayan god.

"Everybody pore over this wall inch by inch," Amy said. "We're looking for a smooth piece of quartz, any size."

Dan and the others inched over the wall with their fingers, eyes close to the stone, searching for anything that might be the riven crystal. Dan finished his section and sat back, his heart sinking. He hadn't found anything unusual. "I've got nothing," he said.

"Me neither," Jake said with a sigh. "Anyone else?"

Amy shook her head. "No. Atticus? You're our last hope."

He looked the most discouraged of all. "It isn't here. I can't understand it. The riven crystal isn't here."

Dan glanced at Amy, who looked like she might break down in frustration. "It doesn't make sense."

"How can it not be here?" Dan asked. "We followed that map to the letter."

"I think this is the wrong temple." Atticus's voice shook. "It's in Tikal somewhere, I'm sure of that. But I must have gone wrong somewhere. . . ."

"This park has two hundred square miles of ruins," Amy said. "We need an exact location or we'll never find the crystal."

"I'll study the book again tonight and figure out where I went wrong. It's the mysterious glyph, the one I couldn't decipher. I'm sure that's what misled me."

He looked at his feet, blinking. Dan was afraid he might cry. Atticus was just a little kid, and they relied on him so much. He hated letting anyone down.

Amy put a reassuring arm around Att's shoulders. "It's all right. It must be that mysterious glyph. We'll figure it out tonight and try again tomorrow."

There was nothing else to do. They crawled out of the ruin and started hiking back through the jungle toward the hotel.

About an hour into the walk back, Dan suddenly had a strange feeling. All this time they'd been alone in the jungle, except for the wild birds and animals—frogs, toads, lizards, snakes . . . Most of the mammals wisely slept during the day. But now the hair on the back of his neck stood up, and he had the strong sense that they were being watched.

He was following Amy, who was leading them back. He touched her arm to get her attention and put his finger to his lips to signal quiet. She and the others instantly froze.

They peered through the dense rain forest. Birds whistled and hooted. There was a cracking sound, like a twig or branch breaking.

Amy's eyebrows rose in alarm.

Dan thought he saw something catch the light and glint through the leaves. Or was that his imagination?

Another *crack*, and a flash of light as the sun hit the watch on a man's wrist.

"They're here," Amy whispered.

Before they could make a move, four large men crashed through the brush, blocking the way forward.

"Run!" Amy shouted.

CHAPTER 9

Amy whirled around and ran back down the path with Dan, Jake, and Atticus at her heels, when four more fighters leaped out of the trees.

"It's an ambush!" Dan yelled.

They were trapped. Thugs in front of them, thugs behind them, and all around them nothing but impenetrable jungle. *How did they find us?* Amy's muscles tensed and her pulse sped, telling her to run, but there was nowhere to go. She felt like a caged tiger. Two of Pierce's men rushed forward and grabbed her. She struggled but their hands were pure muscle, gripping her arms so hard they nearly broke her bones.

Jake was dodging a goon who looked more like a boulder than a man, bald with a big nose mashed against his face. Ducking and swerving, he stayed one step ahead of the thug but couldn't quite lose him. When the fighter finally treed him, Jake jumped up higher, grabbed a branch, and kicked the man in the face—just hard enough to give Jake time to escape.

A soldier went for Atticus, who flattened himself

against the jungle floor and slithered through a narrow opening in the brush, disappearing. Dan ducked and rolled, dodging the soldier who chased him, and dove into the brush after Att. The thugs kicked furiously at the thick vines, ripping them up by the roots like a threshing machine. *Go, Dan and Att, go!* Amy thought. She squirmed in the iron grip of the men holding her. One of them reached for his gun. In a surge of terror and adrenaline she kicked his hand hard enough to hurt him. The gun flew into the air and disappeared in the green.

"Get it!" the other thug ordered. The gunman let go of Amy. Now she had one arm free. She punched the other goon in the stomach, followed by a hard judo chop on his arm and another kick to the groin. The blows had no effect. She might as well have been a fly fighting an elephant.

Jake appeared behind the thug, grabbed a handful of hair, and yanked. Enraged, the man let go of Amy for a split second to turn on Jake. Amy slipped away, and Jake ducked under the fighter's flying fist, managing to escape. "The boys!" Amy said to Jake. She dove into the jungle after Atticus and Dan. Jake followed. Vines and branches scratched her face as she crawled through the brush. She emerged in a clearing and stood. Dan and Atticus jumped out of a hollow tree they'd been hiding in.

"Amy, look up!" Dan shouted, pointing toward the treetops. Perched in a sturdy kapok branch was a wooden platform with a zip line attached to it. Amy didn't know where the zip line led to, and she didn't care. Anyplace was better than this.

"Get up there any way you can!" she told the others. A rickety wooden staircase led to the platform. She grabbed Atticus and pushed him up the stairs, clambering after him. The stairs were too narrow for the muscular men. One of them tried the first step, and it crashed under his weight. Dan and Jake dodged the goons, climbing up the tree that led to the platform and hauling themselves over the top.

Amy grabbed a zip line harness, helped Atticus inside, and gave him a shove. She followed in another harness, with Dan and Jake sliding in close behind her. They whizzed through the jungle, over the fern-covered ruins, past wildly colored birds and flowers, landing on a platform a hundred yards away, where another zip line awaited them.

The soldiers had somehow managed to climb the tree and were zipping down the lines after them without harnesses. They slid along the wire with their hands, wearing only their gloves. *They're relentless*, Amy thought, trying not to be overwhelmed by despair.

The four of them zipped to another platform. Suddenly, about twenty feet from the next platform, Atticus stopped dead. "My harness is stuck!" he shouted.

Amy couldn't stop — she slid right into him. Dan crashed into her, and the weight of them unstuck Att's harness. They zipped the final leg to the next platform.

Jake tumbled on after them. Out of breath, Amy glanced back. The thugs were zooming straight toward them, a hundred feet away, then fifty, twenty. . . .

Up ahead, there was no zip line. Only a suspension bridge made of rope and planks, spanning a deep, dry gorge.

"The goons are right behind us," Dan shouted. "Go!"

Amy stepped tentatively on the bridge, testing its strength. It swayed under her weight. Dan stepped on, causing the bridge to ripple. She looked down. Big mistake. The bottom of the gorge was far, far below, with nothing to land on but rocks.

"Amy, go!" Dan urged her. "They're coming!" She took a breath, then another step. One foot at a time . . .

She started across the bridge, trying to ignore the waves of nausea and dizziness that washed over her. "Eyes up!" Jake instructed. Amy listened, keeping her eyes on the other side of the gorge. She'd made it halfway across, the boys right behind her. The bridge made a sudden huge ripple, swinging over the chasm. The goons had arrived. She gripped the rope sides tighter.

"Hurry!" Dan said. "This thing could snap under the weight of those guys."

Another big ripple as the thugs piled on. Amy's foot slid out from under her. She landed on her backside on a plank of the bridge, then slipped sideways, her legs dangling over the gorge.

"Amy!" Jake cried.

Her hands caught the rope that ran along the side

of the bridge. She dangled over the gorge for a split second before Jake pulled her to safety. She knelt on the bridge, catching her breath, before climbing to her feet and hurrying the rest of the way over the gorge.

They'd all made it safely across the bridge. They ran along a jungle path, only to find themselves at another zip line, this one running over a rushing river.

"I remember the map! This line should lead to the zip line center," Dan cried.

"Good." The zip line center would be crowded with tourists and patrolled by armed park guards. If they could get to the center, they might be safe from Pierce's men, at least for a little while. "Let's go," Amy said.

Jake lifted Atticus into a harness and sent him soaring like a bird over the rushing water. Jake followed to make sure he'd be okay on the other side. They zoomed across the river and disappeared into the trees on their way to the zip line center. Amy glanced back. No sign of the men who'd been chasing them yet. But they were sure to appear any moment. She pushed Dan in front of her. "Go. Now!"

Dan jumped into the harness and slid across the double wire that connected the platform to the other side of the river. At that moment a new thug appeared on the far shore — another one of Pierce's men, coming at them from the other side. The thugs had called for reinforcements. Jake and Atticus had zipped by right before he got there. He spoke into a two-way radio, nodding as if he'd just been told where to go and what to do. Brandishing a machete, he climbed up to a platform in a tree next to the zip line. Then he started hacking at one of the two zip line wires.

Dan was headed straight for him.

Amy's heart jumped to her throat. Dan was halfway across when the top wire that held him snapped.

"Dan!" Amy screamed.

The wire dropped in front of Dan. His harness halted with a jerk and the lower wire drooped low over the river. He dangled above the water rushing over the rocks below, supported by only one wire now, the other in his way, keeping him from sliding forward.

Amy heard thudding footsteps behind her. She turned quickly. The rickety suspension bridge had slowed down the fighters who'd been chasing them—the men were so big they had to cross it carefully, or their weight might break it or sway it so much it would throw them off. But they had finally made it over the bridge and were running toward her down the jungle path.

They'd be on top of her in a matter of minutes.

Across the river, the saboteur hacked at the second wire. Once it broke, the pulleys holding the harness would slide off the wire and Dan would tumble into the river to his death.

"DAN!" she screamed again.

Dan twisted in the harness, looking for Amy. When he found her, they locked eyes. She could read his thoughts, and they were terrible.

This is it, he telegraphed to her. *Good-bye.*

No! Her body jolted with terror, a lightning bolt to the brain.

Without thinking, she jumped into her harness. She'd zip over to Dan, catch him, glide him to safety. . . .

She'd nearly leaped over the water when she caught herself. It wouldn't work. She'd reach Dan halfway over the river, and they'd both be stuck. Half the zip line had been cut. Across the river, the strongman was chopping, chopping, chopping. The second wire weakened, sagging even more.

Dan's body dropped closer to the rushing water, the harness holding him like a noose.

Every nerve, every fiber in Amy's body strained over that river toward her brother. Her brain was on fire, rat-a-tatting, *save him save him how how how?*

She scanned the ground for a life preserver, a float, something she could toss him that might break his fall, but there was nothing. The wire thinned. Dan's body dropped lower. He closed his eyes, his face a mask of terror.

The wire was hair-thin. It was about to break.

Behind her, the thugs were only yards away.

As if in a nightmare, Amy saw what was about to happen. She saw Dan's body fall into the river. She saw his head bash against the rocks, spattering them with blood as his limp, lifeless body washed downstream. . . .

If only he could climb back to her, back on the wire.

But he wasn't strong enough to do that, and anyway, the thugs would be waiting for him there on her side of the river. Or if he could cling to the wire as it broke, and slide down slowly toward the river. But he'd have to be superstrong to do that, at least as strong as Pierce's men, maybe stronger.

A howl of anguish ripped from her body. He was her brother, and she couldn't help him! She was powerless, powerless, power . . .

Power.

In a flash an answer appeared to her. She had all the power she needed. Right there in her backpack.

The serum.

If she were superstrong, she could slide out to him, keep him from falling, ease him down the wire to the edge of the river. . . .

If she were superstrong, and if she acted fast.

The wire sagged lower. In ten seconds, maybe five, it would break. Dan struggled in the harness, trying to claw his way back along the wire toward her, but he wasn't strong enough. He was as helpless as a trapped animal.

Her little brother. Her Dan.

Save Dan, save Dan, save Dan. . . . The words were a drumbeat in her mind. She couldn't think of anything else, couldn't think past that one idea.

She ripped open her pack and found the flask. She tore off the top and drank it down.

CHAPTER 10

There was an agonizing instant when nothing happened, and then power like golden light surged through her veins, energizing her limbs, her hands, her brain. She felt strong, yet light. As if she could leap across the chasm, fifty yards, a hundred. No—she tried to put a brake on her speeding mind; she could jump far, very far, maybe thirty feet, but not that far, not yet. . . .

Concentrate.

Her mind immediately focused on Dan. The thugs surrounded her, but she jumped out of their reach, her legs springing her higher than she thought possible, and grabbed the zip line wire, the one that was being cut on the other side of the river.

Amy made her way along the wire, hand over hand. She reached Dan in a matter of seconds, just as the wire broke. He dropped toward the water as his harness slid off the broken wire. But instead of filling her with terror, the sight of her freefalling brother activated a surge of energy as her arm shot out, grabbing one of Dan's hands just before he fell out of reach.

"Hold on!" she told him. She strained all her muscles to tighten her grasp. The wire tore at the skin on her hand. The momentum of the fall swung them back over the river, back to the side where Pierce's men were waiting. She clung to the wire like Tarzan clinging to a vine. They swooped upward and crashed into the stunned goons waiting for them there, knocking them to the ground.

Dan stared at Amy in shock. "What—?"

"Get on my back," Amy ordered. The zip line wire now dangled down the cliff toward the rushing water. Dan clung to her back like a little kid. She shimmied down the wire, bracing her feet against the cliff.

"Amy, what are you doing?" Dan felt heavy, but she knew she wouldn't drop him unless he let go.

"I've got you. Just hold on tight," she shouted. They made their way down the wire, rappelling against the cliff. She jumped the last twenty feet to the narrow river's edge. He slid off her back. Large rocks dotted the water from one side to the other. She stepped on the first rock, then the next. They were sharp, wet, and slippery. "To the other side! Come on!" she told Dan.

He struggled to follow her across the rocks. Her sense of balance was supersharp—she hardly had to hold on to the rocks as she leaped from one to the next. Dan crouched down, clinging to each boulder as he slowly made his way over the rushing water.

She helped him over the last few rocks until they landed on the other side of the river. Pierce's men watched them helplessly from above, unable to reach them. "What do we do now?" Dan asked. There was nowhere to go but up, nothing on that side but a sheer cliff about thirty feet high.

"We climb."

"But what about—?" Dan pointed at the man with the machete looking down at them.

Amy studied him. He had a machete, but there was only one of him. "We'll deal with him when we get there." She hoisted Dan onto her back again and started scaling the cliff. She stretched to reach a jutting rock, clung to it while her foot found a sturdy hold, and slowly made her way up the face of the cliff.

About three feet below the top of the cliff was a narrow ledge of rock. "Climb off," she told Dan. She left him perched on the ledge. Just above her, the man with the machete was waiting.

Amy hoisted herself to the top of the cliff. The thug raised the machete, ready to strike. She kicked it out of his hand. It fell over the cliff to the river, clanking heavily against the rocks. The thug's jaw dropped open in surprise. Amy knocked him flat with one swift kick to the gut. She reached down to Dan, hauling him up to the top of the cliff.

They ran through the jungle to the zip line center a quarter mile away, where Jake and Atticus were waiting for them. She had to hold herself back so Dan could keep up with her. She felt like a gazelle, as if she could breeze through the jungle for miles and never get tired.

"Are you okay?" Jake asked. "What took you so long?"

"We're fine," Amy said. "We're great." She wasn't even out of breath. She could have kept running, she could have run a marathon without getting tired. She bounced up and down on her toes.

"Amy." Dan was gasping for breath. *"What just HAPPENED?"*

"What do you mean?" The golden energy coursed through her veins. She knew what he meant; in the back of her mind she knew something was wrong, but she couldn't feel it, she could only feel the energy.

"You — you caught me before I fell," Dan said, staring at her in disbelief, as if the strangeness of what had happened was just dawning on him. "You rappelled down a cliff with me on your back. You took on one of Pierce's thugs like it was nothing —"

"What?" Jake asked. "Amy — ?"

She stopped bouncing. She still felt the energy coursing through her veins, shining out of her eyes. But the voice in the back of her mind was getting clearer: *Something is wrong, something is very wrong. . . .*

"I had to do it, Dan," she said. "I couldn't let you die. . . ."

Dan's mouth opened, then closed. *He knows,* she thought. *He knows but he can't say it out loud.* "It was worth it," she said. She was done letting him make her feel guilty for saving him. "I'd do it again."

"What are you talking about?" Jake demanded.

Dan and Atticus stared at her with questions in

their eyes, and fear. "The serum," she told them in a confident voice she didn't recognize as her own. "I had a vial of it with me. Dan was about to die. I had to save him. So . . . I drank it."

"You had it with you?" Dan asked. His features were frozen in shock. "All this time?" She nodded. "And you . . . you took it." He looked down now as if the gravity of what had happened was beginning to weigh on him. "The full-strength serum."

She nodded again. His eyes searched her face as if looking for something—or someone—he'd lost long ago.

Amy recoiled from the look on his face as if it were a blow, the confidence draining away as quickly as it'd appeared. *What have I done?*

"I don't understand," Jake said.

She looked at Dan, and his eyes filled with tears. He fell against her in a long, deep hug. She held him, never wanting to let go. Her little brother, safe in her arms.

Atticus stepped forward and put a small arm around each of them. "What, you guys? What is it?"

Dan just shook his head as if he couldn't speak.

"I took the Cahill serum," Amy explained gravely. "That means I will be the strongest, smartest, most powerful person on earth. For one week."

"And then?" Jake asked.

Dan started sobbing, soaking her T-shirt.

"And then," she said slowly, the gravity of it finally sinking in, hitting her like a blow to the solar plexus, "I will die."

CHAPTER 11

Dan held on to Amy the whole way back to the hotel. He couldn't bring himself to let go. Tears streamed down his face and he couldn't make them stop.

His heart was breaking. He didn't even care how it looked, a thirteen-year-old boy with his arm around his sister's waist, sobbing uncontrollably. Nothing mattered now.

Amy had taken the serum to save him. And now she was going to die.

Maybe dying would have been better than this, the heavy guilt weighing on his heart like a lead blanket. It was his fault that the serum existed at all. His fault that Amy had been secretly carrying it around for safekeeping. His fault that she'd taken it . . .

His fault that she would soon die.

He could feel how the serum had changed her while they walked. Jake and Atticus stumbled down the path like zombies, numb with shock. But Dan could feel Amy holding herself back to keep from running ahead of him. Her skin seemed to hum with energy and power.

He couldn't hold on to her forever. He let her go.

She immediately sprang ahead, almost involuntarily. She hopped up onto a stone fence in one easy leap, then double-back-flipped off.

She turned back to Dan with a sad, apologetic smile. "I've always wanted to do that."

Jake and Atticus watched her blankly, as if they couldn't quite comprehend what was happening. The Amy they knew was no gymnast—especially not at a time like this.

It doesn't seem real to her, Dan thought. *She's feeling the power, the strength . . . but not the poison.*

It didn't quite seem real to him, either.

Back at the hotel, Amy bounced around the room, trying to contain her energy. It might've been comforting—someone that full of life couldn't possibly be *dying*. But Dan could see the emotions playing over her face, bouncing around, too. One minute she looked giddy with power, the next overwhelmed by panic.

Atticus tried to take her hand and lead her into a seat. When that failed, Jake took a more direct approach. "Amy, settle down," he barked. "We've got to concentrate on finding the crystal. The antidote is more important than ever now." His tone was harsh, as if he were furious with Amy, but whenever Dan caught Jake's eye, he could see a flicker of anguish.

"I need to look at those glyphs." Atticus's breath shook as he spoke, but he tried to hide his fear, tried to act as tough as Jake. "Where's Olivia's book, Dan?"

The book. Dan opened his backpack and rummaged through it. "I had it in here when we were attacked. . . ." He searched the pack, then emptied it. "Maybe I put it in my back pocket." He patted his pockets, then pulled them inside out. No book.

"Dan, where is it?" Amy's voice was high and tense.

"I—I don't know." He was beginning to panic, the terror rising from his gut with a bitter, metallic taste.

"Check the pack again," Atticus said.

"I am." Dan double- and triple-checked every corner of his backpack, every pocket. There was no way around it. Olivia's book was gone.

"It must have fallen out of my pocket when I was fighting off Pierce's men," Dan said.

So it was somewhere out there in the jungle . . . the vast jungle where planes could crash and never be found.

The mood in the room settled into a dark gloom. Dan kicked over a chair in a fury.

Amy was dying. And now the book was gone.

He'd done it again. He'd let Amy down. She'd been right to abandon him. He couldn't be counted on to do anything right.

Without the crystal and a perfect antidote recipe, Amy could not be saved. Dan knew the recipe by heart, though some of the more complicated codes had yet to be deciphered. The book was crammed with information that shed light on the recipe — like where to find the exact ingredients. One small mistake and the antidote wouldn't work.

And he'd lost the book. It was his fault.

His sister, who stood before him now so full of life, would be dead in a week. Only seven more days of eye rolls whenever he made a bad joke. 168 hours of ruffling his hair and calling him a dweeb with a smile that meant she wouldn't have him any other way. 10,080 minutes left with his big sister, the one who'd let him sleep in her bed for a year after their parents died, who skipped the first day of seventh grade to sit on a bench next to Dan's elementary school and wave to him during recess. Amy, the only family he had left, gone forever.

The clock was ticking. They still had to stop Pierce from taking over the world. But first they had to save Amy's life.

CHAPTER 12

Off the coast of Maine

After clobbering Galt in their morning karate bout, Cara showered and changed for Round Table. Round Table was a "quiz game" her father had invented, where she and Galt competed to see which of them had the most knowledge of politics and history. Pierce played "moderator," asking the questions. He kept a running tally of points won by each child. At the moment, Galt was beating Cara 110 to 100. But Cara had been beating him lately. She was closing the gap. Maybe today would be the day when she'd pull ahead. And if she did, would her father finally take notice and realize that Cara was as worthy of his attention as Galt?

Cara finished dressing and glanced through her history notes. The facts and figures stuck in her mind so easily now. Her memory had improved while she was taking the power shakes her father had given her, but with the extra punch from Galt's shake, her memory had become photographic.

Galt and her father were waiting for her in Pierce's study. She took her place at the round "game table," which was equipped with little buzzers, just like a real quiz show. *Let the games begin.*

"Are you both ready?" Pierce shuffled through his note cards and trained his icy blue eyes on his children. "All right, Round Table, Round Five. Let's begin. Secret Service Code Names: What is the Secret Service Code Name for Barack Obama?"

Easy one. Cara pressed her buzzer a split second before Galt did. "Renegade."

"Correct. Give me three more code names for bonus points."

"Bill Clinton: Eagle. Richard Nixon: Searchlight. John F. Kennedy: Lancer. Senator Ted Kennedy: Sunburn—" Cara could go on forever.

"Enough." Pierce's voice was stern, but he was smiling. "I only asked for three, Cara."

"You should penalize her a point," Galt said.

"I'm not going to penalize her for doing more than I asked," Pierce said. "You should always strive to do more than is asked of you. That's how you get ahead."

Galt scowled.

"Next question. Name three cities that have hosted the Republican National Convention. Go."

Again Cara was quicker to buzz. "Tampa, 2012; St. Paul, 2008; New York, 2004; Philadelphia, 2000—"

"Showoff," Galt grumbled.

"Extra credit for knowing the years. Good job,

Cara." Pierce noted Cara's points on a score sheet and shuffled his question cards. "Lightning round. This one's for the losers. I'll name a president, and you tell me the name of the candidate he beat. Ready? Dwight D. Eisenhower." Cara buzzed. "Cara."

"Adlai Stevenson." *Give me something challenging*, Cara thought. *This is too easy.*

"George W. Bush in 2000. Cara."

"Al Gore *and* Ralph Nader," Cara said.

"Ralph Nader! Green Party!" Galt shouted out.

"Too late, Galt. George H. W. Bush. Cara."

"Michael Dukakis."

"Right. Um . . . Rutherford B. Hayes. Galt."

"Samuel J. Tilden," Galt said.

"Score one for Galt." Pierce noted their scores. Of course Galt would get Rutherford B. Hayes—that was his favorite president. Because his name was Galt Rutherford Pierce, after his father.

They played for another half hour. Galt managed to score a few more points, but Cara beat him in the end.

"Cara has pulled ahead," Pierce announced after adding up their scores. "It's now 157 for Cara, 123 for Galt. Nice job, Cara. And as a reward for your impressive performance, you'll be going to Washington with me tomorrow."

Galt jumped to his feet. "What!? You said I could go with you!"

"I think the most politically astute child should be the one who accompanies me while I'm meeting with

Congress," Pierce said, nailing Galt with a hard stare. "Don't you agree, Galt? It only makes sense."

Galt was fuming and frustrated. Cara could practically feel the heat of his rage coming off his skin.

"Thank you, Dad." She stood up to go. "I'll start packing."

"Ask your mother to help you," Pierce called after her. "She knows the right things to wear in Washington."

Cara fumed as she walked up the plushly carpeted stairs to her room. Her father wouldn't have worried about what Galt was going to wear. Was he taking her to Washington because she was smart, as an aide? Or as an ornament, like her mother?

He still favors Galt, Cara realized. Her father thought Cara's recent success was a fluke, just a temporary setback for her brother. *Deep down*, Cara thought bitterly, *in spite of everything I've done, my dad thinks I'm a carbon copy of Mom—basically, a ditz.*

I'll show him.

Cara's mother knocked on her bedroom door later that day. "Would you like to go shopping with me this afternoon, honey?" Debi Ann asked. "Your father told me that he's taking you to Washington with him! That's exciting. There are going to be more and more of these public appearances, and you'll need some new dresses."

Cara knew the kind of dresses her mother wanted

to buy her. They were expensive, neat, and always had some little-girlish detail—a white Peter Pan collar, maybe, or a bow at the waist. Perfect for a candidate's daughter. But utterly ridiculous.

"Can't you just order a few things in my size?"

"Of course, dear." Her mother hated conflict, and she must have known from past experience that a shopping trip with Cara would be one long argument. "Your father said you were a whiz at Round Table this morning." She looked down at her perfect pink manicure, as if she were afraid to meet Cara's eye. As if she were intimidated by her own daughter.

"Thanks, Mom." She could barely look at her mother these days. Debi Ann got this pained, deer-in-the-headlights expression that drove Cara crazy. If only her mother would stand up for herself. But Cara couldn't really blame her. How could anyone stand up to her father?

Debi Ann Pierce sat at the pristine white desk in her pristine white study. This was where she signed the notes her secretary wrote for her, thank-you notes to the wives of visiting dignitaries, get-well cards to important people who were sick, checks to the many charities she supported. She didn't really need a study all to herself, but they had the space, and so here she spent her days, sitting alone, worrying.

Lately her worries had settled on Cara. Cara had changed recently. It was surprising enough when her slightly awkward daughter began excelling at tennis, waterskiing, judo, karate . . . pretty much any sport she tried. She seemed to become a natural athlete almost overnight. Galt, too, though he'd been more athletic than Cara as a young child.

Lately, the children's talents struck Debi Ann as more than just surprising — they were astonishing. Unbelievable. And they made Debi Ann wonder what exactly was going on right here under her own roof.

If Rutherford caught her snooping . . . Debi Ann shuddered. She didn't know what he'd do. She hated to think about it. Yes, she was his wife. But that wouldn't stop him from hurting her if she got in his way. She might as well be a total stranger as far as he was concerned. Or a mosquito, something small and annoying that he could swat away without a thought — and squash if it tried to sting him.

All he cared about were his ambitions. Power. Debi Ann was sure Pierce hadn't felt anything like "love" for anyone — not even for her or the children — in a long time. Not since the woman no one was allowed to name.

So why should she honor his wishes? If she had to trail along in his wake, she wanted to know where they were going.

CHAPTER 13

Tikal, Guatemala

"It's gone," Jake said, shaking his head in disbelief. "It's like the jungle just swallowed it up."

Dan, Jake, and Amy had gone back into the jungle to search for Olivia's lost book, retracing their steps futilely, while Atticus tried to figure out where the riven crystal was.

Dan hunched his shoulders. He looked tense, coiled tight. Amy wanted to comfort him, to let him know she didn't blame him for losing the book, but he shied away whenever she came close. At one point, he'd actually shuddered, as if she were already dead and he had just brushed against a corpse.

He caught her watching him. "What?" he asked, his voice strangely flat.

"Nothing," she said. "Just hope you're okay."

"I'm fine," he said, avoiding her eyes. She could feel him shutting down, pulling away as if trying to get a head start on his grief. Or was he *punishing* her for dying? For taking drastic action to save *his* life? Could he possibly be that ungrateful? And yet . . . she understood. If the burden had been too much for him before, it was greater than ever now.

No one said a word on the long walk back to the hotel. The silence was thicker than the heat, heavy with all the thoughts they were afraid to say aloud.

"Any luck with the glyph, Att?" Dan asked when they returned to the hotel.

Atticus shook his head. "I've checked all the hieroglyphs that have been deciphered so far, but this one isn't there. I've even tried reenacting a *pok-a-tok* game with these palm nuts to see if it triggers any ideas. . . . Amy, what does this glyph look like to you?"

Amy sat down with Atticus and focused on the symbol. Maybe now, with her mind sharpened by the power of the serum, she could crack the code. Despite the grave faces surrounding her, she felt invincible. When she focused on distances it was like looking through a telescope. She could spot a worm in a bird's beak miles away. Her vision in the dark was like looking through night goggles. She'd been in great shape before she took the serum, but she'd had to work hard for every muscle. Now, for the first time in her life, bookish Amy Cahill, denizen of the library, was a natural athlete.

She had to keep reminding herself why she felt so strong, and when she remembered, her mood plummeted. The serum was doing this to her. The very thing that made her feel so good now would soon kill her.

But that didn't feel real. Death seemed impossible. She knew in her mind that the serum was fatal, but she couldn't feel it in her body, which was so full of energy and life. It was like carrying a time bomb inside her body, only she misheard the ticking of the bomb as the beating of her heart.

The crystal . . . focus on the crystal. She trained her eyes on the glyph. The bottom part of it had a squar-ish shape with rounded corners and inside it a smaller square and two horizontal lines like dashes. On top of the main square were three vertical rectangles.

"They almost look like panels," she said. "Or — what if the square was a man's face, with two lines for eyes . . . and the top part was a headdress?"

Suddenly, there was a tap at the window. Startled, Amy jumped up and whirled around, leg in the air and fists clenched, ready to defend against an attack. She was about to kick through the window when she saw a small, furry black creature crouched on the sill, staring at the nuts Atticus had left on the table.

"Relax, Amy," Jake said. "It's just a howler monkey."

Amy let her hands fall to her sides. *Breathe, breathe . . .* The monkey knocked on the window again and hopped up and down as if it were laughing at her. She looked more closely at it. "Jake, that's not a howler monkey. It's a spider monkey."

"What?"

"You can tell by the reddish fur on its upper body. Anyone who knew anything about the native fauna of Guatemala would see the difference easily."

She heard the contempt in her voice and saw the flash of hurt surprise on Jake's face. "My mistake," he said.

She opened her mouth to apologize, but another thought zipped through her brain. *He's smart, but he's not a Cahill, and he never will be. He'll never be able to keep up with me and Dan. Why doesn't he just take his little brother and go back to Rome?*

"Amy, it's just a monkey," Dan said.

"Just a monkey? Every detail matters! You know that as well as I do, Dan."

Dan, Jake, and Atticus were all staring at her with worry on their faces. And fear. Amy felt a stab of pain at the sight of them. She wanted to melt into the floor and slip away like mercury. They loved her, all three of them. And she loved them. They were working themselves to the bone to save her life, and she couldn't keep herself from snapping at them. The contempt she'd felt drained away in a rush, replaced by remorse. "Jake, I'm sorry—"

Her phone buzzed—Nellie. Amy was grateful for the distraction. She transferred the call to her laptop so they could all see her and talk to her. Amy was still startled every time she saw Nellie with plain brown hair—no crazy colors, no neon skunk stripes. Yet although she looked shockingly different, she still sounded like the same old Nellie, which was more than Amy could say for herself.

"What's up, kiddos?" Nellie asked. "I've got some

news. Pony confirms that Debi Ann Pierce is Deborah Starling."

"Why didn't we know that before?" Amy asked, working hard to keep her voice calm and measured.

"Pierce had any connection to the names 'Starling' or 'Cahill' wiped from his Internet history," Nellie explained.

"I thought that was impossible," Atticus said.

"It's not easy," Nellie said. "Pony says April May did it."

"If she's still working for Pierce, it would explain the ambush," Amy said.

"What ambush?" Nellie cried in alarm.

"They swarmed us when we went to find the riven crystal," Amy explained.

"And Dan almost got killed," Atticus added before Amy could shush him.

"What?" Nellie shrieked. "Dan, are you okay? Put your face close to the camera so I can see you clearly."

Dan pushed his face at the camera on Amy's laptop. "I'm fine, Nellie. Don't worry. Amy saved my butt."

"Don't worry? You were almost killed! What happened?"

Amy struggled with the warring impulses inside her. The slightest threat to her kiddos and Nellie went into battle mode. She'd done so much to protect them, made so many sacrifices. Amy felt protective of *her* now, wanting to spare her this blow. But Nellie deserved to know the truth. She needed to know.

"Calm down, Nellie," Amy said, keeping her voice steady. Nellie had started pacing in front of the computer screen, unable to stand the suspense. "Pierce's men ambushed us in the jungle, and they tried to cut a zip line while Dan was on it—"

"Dangling over a river—" Dan put in.

"—but I rescued him, and we all got away safely. That's the good news."

Nellie's eyes narrowed. "What's the bad news?"

Dan glanced at Amy, and she knew he was trying to postpone the inevitable, too. "I lost Olivia's book," he confessed, stalling for time. "It fell out of my pocket while we were fighting the soldiers, and we can't find it."

"Okay." Nellie nodded. "Okay. Okay. That's bad. That's very bad, but as long as my two kiddos are safe . . ."

"It's not that simple," Amy said. "Dan was—he was about to die. He was dangling over a river. He would have fallen and smashed against the rocks, if—if—"

Nellie stopped pacing. "If what?"

Dan looked at Amy. She shook her head. She couldn't do it.

"Spit it out, kids," Nellie said.

"Amy took the serum." Dan's shoulders hunched as he spoke. Amy could see the coil of anger and pain inside him tighten. "The original, undiluted serum. A full dose. That's how she had the strength to save me."

Nellie blinked. "What are you talking about? How could Amy take the—?"

"I had a vial of it," Amy said. "Sammy made it for me."

As the news sank in, Nellie's features contorted in pain. Amy knew she was watching her friend's heart break.

Nellie pressed her palms against her eyes, then dropped her head on the table in front of her. Finally, she lifted her head and wiped her eyes. "I am not going to let you die." Her voice had grown fierce. "You won't die. All we need is the antidote. Did you get the crystal?"

Atticus frowned. "Still working on it."

"Wait." Amy hovered by Atticus's shoulder and looked at the glyph. From a slight distance she saw it differently—more clearly. "I know what those vertical rectangles remind me of. A mirror."

Atticus tilted his head, studying the symbol. "A mirror?"

"You know, that three-way kind they have in store dressing rooms, or on a vanity table?"

The three boys were giving her blank looks, but on the computer screen Nellie perked up. "I know what you mean. The kind with three panels, so you can see yourself in front and from both sides at the same time."

"Right!" Amy said. "Does that help you, Atticus?"

"A mirror . . ." Atticus picked up his laptop and started searching for something. "That sounds familiar." A few minutes later he jotted something on the paper. For the first time all day, Atticus smiled.

"Amy, I think you cracked it."

CHAPTER 14

Washington, DC

"What this country needs is more democracy." Pierce was standing in front of the Lincoln Memorial with his daughter, Cara, by his side, surrounded by a select group of US senators. He wasn't supposed to be giving a speech, but the press was there, so why not?

"And what does a democracy need to grow? Strong leadership." Pierce patted the giant stone pedestal underneath the statue of Abraham Lincoln as senators nodded and clapped around him. "This country hasn't had a real leader in years. What we need is a true patriot—someone who understands that America comes first, and every other country should bow down to our power!"

Cara was amazed at the enthusiastic applause. How did her father get away with this stuff?

"Excuse me, Mr. Pierce." One reporter waved a pen to get his attention. "Is that how you define democracy? It sounds more like a dictatorship to me."

"You, madam, are not a patriot!" Pierce said with a dangerous smile. "Get that reporter's name," he muttered to one of his bodyguards. "I'll see that she's fired."

Whoa, Cara thought.

Cara was used to her father's ruthless tactics—that's why he had a real shot of winning the election. But she'd never really stopped to think what would happen *after* he was sworn in. Who would be president? The nonstop charm machine the public saw? Or the J. Rutherford Pierce that only Cara, Galt, and their mother knew, a man who cared about power more than anything, more than his own family.

They finished their tour of the great monuments of Washington with a state dinner at the Capitol. While waiters served them roast beef and potatoes, Cara steered the conversation in a direction she knew her father would like: foreign policy. He had just been touring the capitals of Europe, making sure to act as boorishly American as possible wherever he went, and he had lots of funny stories to tell of uptight prime ministers looking like fools around a laid-back American.

Laid-back. Cara wanted to laugh. It was the last phrase she'd use to describe her father. But he'd become a genius at being whoever people wanted to be. The perfect candidate.

"So I said to the chancellor, I said, 'Well, Helmut, the problem with your country is you spend too darn much money on silly things like art. If you spent the money you give to the arts on your military, you wouldn't need to come crying to Uncle Sam every time some nut in a banana republic sneezes.'"

The senators at the table laughed appreciatively, but one aide looked a little troubled. "It might be okay to joke around with our allies in Europe," he said. "But what about someone like the president of Iran? How would you handle diplomacy with him?"

"Son, what you've got to understand is these leaders are people just like you and me. They can boast and bluster all they want, but if you show them you're not impressed and treat them like a good ol' boy, or *girl*," Pierce added with a wink, "then you've got them eating out of your hand like a gerbil."

What is with the wink? Cara was annoyed. Then, as the table broke up laughing, she felt something bony knock against her shin, and the senator sitting next to Pierce cried, "Ow! Pierce, did you just kick me?"

It was quick, but Cara caught it—something she'd never seen on her father's face before. A flash of panic. It was gone so fast she thought she might have imagined it. But she hadn't imagined that her father had kicked both her and the senator under the table, and he couldn't have meant to.

Pierce laughed again, coolly this time. "I'm sorry about that, Senator. You must forgive me. It's just that the president of Iran makes me so darn mad I could kick someone—and you just happened to get in the way!"

More laughter. The offended senator seemed to accept Pierce's jokey explanation. But Cara knew it was a cover-up. Her father's leg had jerked against his will. For a split second, in front of all those politicians, he had lost control over himself.

Her father. Losing control.

She'd once thought that was impossible. But maybe it wasn't.

She didn't know for sure what had caused that spasm, but she had a theory—and it scared her. Her father had been drinking those special power shakes for longer than she had, and he took a bigger dose of whatever that stuff was he put in them. But what *was* that stuff? She knew it enhanced her physical and mental powers—but what else did it do?

What was it doing to *her*?

She found herself staring at her fingers, touching her knee, checking to see if her legs were doing any involuntary shaking. So far she was okay. But she felt the other changes, the good changes—the speed, the wit, the easy charm—and thought, *Those things don't come free.*

Someday she'd have to pay a price.

"It's time these so-called 'heads of state' learned what *real* leadership is. *American* leadership," Pierce continued.

Cara shuddered as another question iced down her spine. *What price would the world have to pay?*

CHAPTER 15

Tikal, Guatemala

Amy marveled at Atticus. The boy knew his stuff, and he wasted no time. That afternoon he led them to a group of structures just south of the Mundo Perdido, or the Lost World, the oldest part of Tikal. "This is called the *Mural de los Jugadores*," he explained, showing them an excavated mural from about 370 B.C. "*The Ball Players Mural*. It depicts an epic ball game between two sets of characters in Mayan mythology: the Hero Twins and the Lords of the Underworld."

The western sector of the mural showed three men in ceremonial dress facing some brick-like patterns that Atticus thought represented a ball court. The figures on the eastern sector of the mural were damaged, so that only their feet were visible.

"This is one of the Hero Twins." He pointed to a man in the mural wearing a headband and ornaments made of bones. "The Lords of the Underworld were painted on the damaged side of the mural, so we can't see them.

But one of them was called the Lord of the Mirrors."

"Mirrors," Amy said. "Like in Olivia's book."

"I suspect that glyph was once part of this mural—on the damaged side," Atticus said. "And in terms of decoding the map that leads to the riven crystal, it fits with the *pok-a-tok* theme."

"But what does it mean?" Dan asked.

"I think it's code for *opposite*," Atticus said.

"Like a mirror image," Amy said.

"Right. If I redraw the map as it would look in a mirror, it would send us to the opposite side of the park," Atticus said.

"To another unexcavated temple—" Jake added.

"—where the crystal should be," Dan finished.

"Let's go find it." Amy barked the words like an order.

"I think Atticus should redraw the map first, so we don't get lost," Jake said.

"We won't get lost. I can see it all in my head—the

whole park." Amy's mind was supercharged, thinking a thousand miles a second. She passed through the entrance to a house in the Mundo Perdido, shaped like a serpent's maw, muttering to herself, thinking out loud, twirling in place to let the others catch up.

"Amy, you're making me dizzy," Dan said with worry in his voice. "I feel like I'm on the teacup ride at Disneyland."

"I'm thinking," Amy replied, but the truth was she couldn't stand still. The serum was coursing through her veins, energizing her, calling her muscles to action. Her muscles demanded something to do. It was a strange feeling for a girl who could normally sit reading in a window seat for hours without pausing to look up.

She felt a twitch in her pinky finger and stopped twirling. She stared at the finger. It twitched again. Strange, but nothing to be too worried about . . .

But then, suddenly, her stomach churned. Probably from spinning around and around the way she'd been doing. She stood perfectly still, trying to calm her nerves.

"You stopped twirling, finally," Dan said. "Thank you."

She swallowed and nodded. Dan's face blurred. She blinked, trying to clear her vision. His skin, his hair, his eyes—everything looked yellowish, as if she were gazing through a yellow lens. Or was that her imagination?

"Amy, what's wrong?" Atticus asked.

She blinked again, and her vision cleared. The

yellowing and blurring were gone. She touched her pinky with the other hand. Steady. "I'm fine," she said. "Perfectly okay."

But everyone knew she wasn't fine. She had six days to live. And the side effects that would kill her had begun.

"Shake it off, Amy," Jake said with the same mix of fear and irritation that had colored everything he'd directed toward her since she took the serum, as if all she had to do to stop dying was "put her mind to it." Her supersharp mind picked up the angry flash in his eyes, perceived the way they lightened for a split second from gray blue to azure as clearly as if it had happened in slow motion.

"Shake what off? I told you I'm fine."

The three boys stood awkwardly around Amy, afraid to touch her. She was at once very strong and very delicate, as if an accidental jostle might break her, or one wrong word could set her off, make her snap at them with a fierceness she couldn't quite control.

"The crystal," she reminded them. "We're going to go find it tonight."

"What about Pierce's men?" Atticus asked. "What if they're spying on us? What if they ambush us again?"

Poor Att. He'd been through a lot for a little kid. Being chased around the world by Pierce's men must have felt like living in a bad dream where the bogeyman was always after him.

Her brain suddenly lit up—she could actually feel

the neurons firing—with a brilliant idea.

Pierce's men were always in the way. Always the obstacle that kept Amy from her goal. The answer was obvious. Get rid of them.

Amy turned to face the boys. "We'll set a trap."

Jake looked alarmed. "Set a trap for who?"

"Pierce's men." Amy stalked forward again, barely giving the others a chance to keep up. "Think about it. They're trying to kill us. We spend a lot of time and energy fighting them off, running away from them, just trying to stay alive. If we didn't have to do all that, we could make the antidote a whole lot faster."

"I wish they'd shrivel up and crawl into a hole, too," Dan said. "But that's not going to happen. Those dudes aren't going anywhere."

"That's why we have to trap them—the ones who are here in Tikal, at least. Then we'll be free to find the crystal and the book without worrying and watching our backs all the time."

"Trap them how?" Atticus asked.

"I'm working on that," Amy said. "I'm thinking some kind of cage, or a pit . . . a very deep pit, so deep they'd never get out." She jumped up on a high wall, walked along it as if it were a balance beam, and jumped off as neatly as a gymnast, all without giving it a thought. Her mind seemed to work better if her body was kept busy this way.

She turned to see how far behind her they'd fallen. They'd stopped, all three of them. They were standing in the middle of the path, staring at her as if she were a lunatic. "Nothing will go wrong," she insisted. "We do away with them. It makes sense. It makes *more* than sense." That was how things seemed to Amy then, bigger, better, more. . . . It was part of the way the serum acted on her. Brilliant ideas flew through her mind so fast she barely had time to catch them. There were so many! It was amazing, but it made it hard to relax. Impossible to relax, actually. Luckily, she never felt tired. She started walking again, but the three boys still didn't move. "What?" she demanded.

"You want to trap people in a pit?" Jake asked. "A pit so deep they can't climb out?"

"If they fell into a pit that deep, they could break their legs," Dan said.

"And then what?" Jake prodded. "You'd leave them there in the pit? With no food or water, and possibly broken legs . . ."

". . . to die in the jungle?" Dan said. She could hear the real question in his voice: *Amy, are you in there?*

Atticus said nothing. He just held back, as if he were a little bit afraid of her.

Now she knew why she'd never thought of this plan before.

It was murder.

She started to tremble. Atticus walked slowly up to her and put his arms around her the way a lost child hugs his mother. "Oh, Att," she whispered, stroking his hair. "I don't know what's happening to me."

CHAPTER 16

Trilon Laboratories
Delaware

"Excuse me, Dr. Gormey. I have a question for you."

Nellie bristled. Her coworker, Dr. Brent Beckelheimer, was a brilliant chemist but supremely annoying. She knew she'd have a problem with him the minute she noticed how he'd decorated his workspace: with a collection of miniature garden gnomes. Just the sight of him made Nellie want to scream. Amy was dying. The kiddos needed Nellie. Dr. Beckelheimer was wasting her time.

Her work at the lab was critical. She knew that. But she felt a magnetic pull south toward Guatemala. All she wanted to do was throw her lab coat on the floor, drive 190 miles per hour to the airport, and go save Amy.

Instead she was stuck in The Middle of Nowhere, Delaware, dealing with buffoons like Dr. Beckelheimer.

She'd assumed, since she was his boss, that she'd be

able to avoid him, but he was strangely sticky, always hovering around. Now he leaned against the door of her office, just off the main lab, where she was supervising a team of chemists who were trying to solve the problem of drug side effects. Her research group had started as a cover operation, but there was a new sense of urgency in the lab and everyone was now working on a mysterious new project. Nellie had a good idea what this mysterious project was, of course, and working on it directly gave her a little more access to top secret information. It made it harder than ever for Nellie to camouflage her total ignorance of organic chemistry, though.

The drug they were studying — though the other scientists weren't aware of it — was the Cahill serum. The side effects they were trying to cure included something called Buccoglossal Syndrome, or involuntary movements of the body.

Nellie knew why they were trying to get rid of Buccoglossal Syndrome. She'd seen the footage of Pierce with the queen of England on TV, and she recognized an involuntary movement when she saw one, no matter how cleverly Pierce had tried to cover it up. But she had to play along, stay friendly with the others to keep them from suspecting that she had infiltrated the company and was basically a corporate spy. "Yes, Dr. Beckelheimer? I only have a second."

"I noticed this chemical compound has a piperazine ring, which interacts with proteins in the body. . . ."

Nellie tensed up and tuned out as he spoke. She had no idea what he was talking about, and she knew from hard experience that hearing more would not help. ". . . when the receptor DRD2 is present; it causes yellow vision instead." Was he still talking?

What about death? she thought. *Have you figured out how to cure that particular side effect?* "Do you think there's a connection?"

"Um . . ." Nellie spun around in her fancy desk chair, tapping a pencil against her teeth. She didn't understand the question, obviously. "Are you asking if there's a connection between yellow vision and Osso Buco Syndrome?"

Whoops. She could tell from Dr. Beckelheimer's stiff, condescending smile that she'd said something wrong. "Did you just say 'Osso Buco Syndrome'?"

"Did I?" Shoot. Osso buco was an Italian meat dish she'd been learning to prepare at cooking school in Boston before she got roped into going undercover at this drug factory.

His eyes narrowed. "I assume you meant Buccoglossal Syndrome."

"Very good. I'm glad to see you know your stuff. Back to work. We've both got a lot to do."

She tried her best to look stern and forbidding, an intimidating boss. It wasn't easy. But it was true that she had a lot of work to do. Nellie had been ordered to write a report synthesizing the biochemists' most recent findings on the side effects of the serum. She told herself not to freak out. *It's like a book report,* she thought. *No different.*

That would have been true if she'd understood any of the "book" she'd read. She focused on an interesting side effect Sammy had noticed—that in late stages the serum could cause Xanthopsia, or—hey, look at that!—yellow vision, just like Dr. Beckelheimer had been saying. Nellie had heard a theory that the painter Vincent van Gogh had suffered from yellow vision, which had a big influence on the coloring of his paintings. She wrote about this in her report, trying to make a case that maybe yellow vision wasn't always such a bad thing. Maybe they could market the drug as something that *promoted* yellow vision, she suggested. The ads could say something like: *You, too, could paint like Vincent van Gogh!*

Or maybe not.

She stayed late working on her report, but Dr. Beckelheimer was still busy working when she left. She passed him on her way out.

"Good night, Dr. Beckelheimer."

"Good night, Dr. Gormey." He had his eye glued to the eyepiece of his microscope. He didn't look up as she left.

The next morning she was called into her supervisor's office. Dr. Stevens didn't look pleased.

"Dr. Gormey, what's the meaning of this?" He waved a sheath of papers in her face. She caught a glimpse of *Vincent van Gogh*.

Beckelheimer. That smug gnome-lover had printed out her report and turned it in to Dr. Stevens before it was ready. He was out to get her.

"Is that my report on Buccoglossal Syndrome?" At least she'd gotten the term right this time.

"Yes, it is. And it's a travesty. I wouldn't even call this science."

"I wasn't finished with it yet, sir. But—may I see it?"

"Certainly." Dr. Stevens handed her the papers. Nellie glanced through it. She couldn't admit to him that she'd written it—he was right. The person who wrote this was clearly not a biochemist. *A marketing genius, maybe, but not a scientist.* And if she was exposed as a fraud, she'd be lucky just to be fired. "This is very serious," Nellie said, pasting her most concerned expression on her face. "May I ask where you got it?"

"Never mind how I got it. The person who brought it to my attention has been concerned for some time that you are not qualified for your job. And based on this report, he's right."

"Dr. Stevens, I didn't write this report. Someone is trying to frame me."

"Dr. Beckelheimer showed it to me. He's one of our best scientists. I trust him completely."

"You do?" Nellie raised one of her eyebrows as high as it would go, so Dr. Stevens wouldn't miss the hint.

"I happen to know he's not trustworthy at all."

"That is a serious allegation, Dr. Gormey. Do you have proof?"

"Let's just say I can convince you that Dr. Beckelheimer is a crackpot. Give me until lunchtime."

"All right. You have until lunchtime. But if you don't convince me, I'll report you."

"That won't be necessary," Nellie said. "You'll see."

She marched to her office and let out a deep breath. All this bluffing was taking a toll on her. A minute to breathe, and she went back into action. She took out her cell. "Pony, I've got a job for you," she said when he answered. "And I think it's going to be pretty easy."

"Anything for you, pretty schoolmarm."

"What? Pony, did you just call me a schoolmarm?"

"I meant *Nellie*, of course. Nellie."

"Pony, are you doing your digital cowboy thing again?"

Silence. She had her answer.

"I like you, Pony. But you need to get out more. Not yet, though. First get me what I need."

"I'm on it like white on rice."

Within an hour, Pony sent Nellie a dozen photos of Dr. Brent Beckelheimer participating in his unusual weekend activity: gnoming. Unlike most gnomers, Dr. Beckelheimer didn't steal people's garden gnomes and pose for pictures with them. He collected them and dressed up as one in his spare time. Beckelheimer's costume was a green velvet three-piece suit, shiny black shoes, a white beard, and wire-rim glasses, topped with a jolly green velvet cap. And was that belly padding?

No. Dr. Beckelheimer didn't need belly padding.

There was plenty of documentation. Nellie got to work printing out the most embarrassing photos.

"Thank you, Pony."

"Any time, goddess. Next time give me something a little bit challenging, would ya?"

"Don't worry, Pony. Something challenging will come along. It always does."

She gave Dr. Beckelheimer a warm smile as she passed his workstation on the way to Dr. Stevens's office. Dr. Beckelheimer nodded back warily. "Oh, you sense that I'm up to something?" Nellie muttered under her breath. "You're darn right I'm up to something. Wait until you find out. . . ."

Dr. Stevens was in a meeting, so she left the photos on his desk with a note. *I don't care what anyone does in his spare time*, she wrote. *But our work here is very sensitive, and I don't think we should risk letting it get into the hands of someone who may be—how shall I put this?—unstable.*

Nellie felt a little bad. She really *didn't* care what people did in their spare time, as long as it didn't hurt anyone. Beckelheimer's gnome obsession seemed harmless, but his other extracurricular activities—trying to expose her as a fraud—were not.

Half an hour later, there was a commotion in the lab.

Two security guards appeared at Dr. Beckelheimer's workstation.

"Sir, we're escorting you from the building. Please get your personal things and come with us."

"What?" Dr. Beckelheimer protested. "What is this? What did I do?"

"Take that up with personnel. We've been ordered to escort you from the building. Please do not take any files or other property of Trilon Laboratories."

Nellie didn't dare leave her office to watch Beckelheimer go. She didn't want to bait him. This wasn't about payback. *Okay, maybe a little bit.* But the most important thing was that she should stay in the good graces of the company—so she could take them down and help her kiddos.

Once things quieted down, Dr. Stevens called her into his office. "Nice work, Dr. Gormey. For helping us weed out dangerous characters, I've decided to promote you to vice president in charge of biochemical research."

"Vice president? Me? I'm honored." *Imagine that*, she thought. *Me, Nellie Gomez—I mean, Nadine Gormey—vice president of a drug company! Now that's something to brag about at my next high school reunion.*

"Keep up the good work," Dr. Stevens said.

"Thank you, Dr. Stevens. I will."

She planned to work harder than ever—just not in the way Dr. Stevens expected her to.

CHAPTER 17

Tikal, Guatemala

They'd spent the whole day searching for Olivia's book, to no avail. Now it was two o'clock in the morning, everyone else was asleep, but Amy was wide awake and pacing, thinking.

Five days to go.

Her thoughts raced in circles like a dog chasing its tail. The antidote. She needed the antidote. Yet for every pang of guilt she felt looking in Dan's eyes, there was a part of her that hoped she'd never take it. When she wasn't reeling from the side effects of the serum, she felt like she would live forever. Why would she want that feeling to end? No way would anything kill her, much less a few silly drops of liquid. She had a lifetime of accomplishments ahead of her. There were books practically writing themselves in her fingertips. Computer programs begging to burst forth from her brain. Her muscles were quivering for a chance to prove themselves in a triathlon, or on a trek up Everest! Taking a helicopter up like she and Dan had done didn't count; she was itching to do it properly—without oxygen!

She stopped short. That didn't make sense. The serum was poison. It was killing her. She'd seen with her own eyes what the serum had done to Ian's mother, Isabel Kabra. She'd felt the tremors.

So where were these thoughts coming from? It was as if her own mind were working against her, sabotaging her. Were these her own genuine thoughts—or were they produced by the serum?

There was a soft knock on her door. She froze. Should she pretend to be asleep?

Before she had time to jump into bed and pull up the covers, Jake opened the door. "Amy—? I thought I heard you walking around in here."

He let himself in and shut the door.

"Did I say you could come in?" she snapped. "I didn't say—"

"Shhh." He pressed a finger against his lips. "You'll wake the boys."

"What do you want? It's the middle of the night."

"I know it's the middle of the night. What I want to know is why you're still up. Can't you sleep?"

She sighed and sat down on her bed. What was the point of lying to him? He already knew the truth. "No. I haven't slept since I took the serum."

His eyes widened. "Amy, I know every second is crucial right now, but you need to rest."

"Why? I've got nothing but energy. I've got five days to live. Might as well make the most of them," she joked lamely.

"Yeah, let's fly to Vegas, take the penthouse suite, bet everything you've got on roulette, and live the high life. One last blast before —" He couldn't finish the joke. The reality was too grim.

She tried to keep the banter going. "Teasing me about my imminent demise," she said. "That's sweet of you."

He gave a rueful smile. "You know me. Mr. Hearts and Flowers."

"Ha. Yeah. Always the romantic."

He reached for the doorknob. "Look, are you going to go to sleep or not? That's all I came in for."

"Yes. I'll sleep," she lied. "Don't worry about me." He just looked at her. "Don't say anything to Dan," she added. "About me not sleeping, I mean. I don't want him to worry, either."

"As if he could help it," Jake said. "I'll say what I want to Dan. I don't take orders from you." A few days ago, his words would've stung, but there was no malice in his tone.

"Hey, Jake?" she called as he turned to the door.

He twisted back around. "Yeah?"

"If something does happen to me, you'll take care of him, right? You're so great with Atticus, and Dan will need someone who . . ." She trailed off as Jake's face grew pale. "Never mind. I shouldn't have said anything."

Jake pressed his lips together for a moment before he spoke. "Of course I will. That goes without saying. But it won't be necessary. We're going to find the ingredients. We'll get you the antidote." He took a step forward, and for a second it looked like he was about to extend his hand, but then his arm fell back to his side. After everything she'd done to him, nothing short of a helicopter crash could induce Jake to touch her.

"Just get some rest. You'll feel better tomorrow." He left the room and shut the door.

She knew he was right. She needed rest. She had to keep herself together.

She was the leader. She was in charge.

If she fell apart, so would everything else.

She woke up in the dark, feeling hot and sweaty. What time was it? She looked around for the glow-in-the-dark clock dial but couldn't see it. She couldn't see anything; the darkness was so thick she could almost feel it, she could smell its musty odor.

She lay back and closed her eyes, hoping this terrible feeling, whatever it was, would go away. Sweat poured off her forehead. Why was she so terribly hot? She sat up in a panic. Fire! It must be fire. She thought of her parents, the fire that had killed them both. Could someone want her to die the same way?

Pierce . . .

She jumped out of bed. She had to warn Dan, to save him, to get him out of the burning hotel. She fumbled through the inky darkness, looking for the door. Then she stopped. She heard something. The roar of the fire? No, it was lower, more ominous. A growl.

Was someone in the room with her? Frantically, she spun around. "Who's there?" she shouted.

No one answered. She froze, listening. Silence.

Pierce's men, she thought. *They've come to get me. To stop me before I can stop them!*

Another sound broke the silence. More growling. *That sound isn't human*, she realized. *It's a jaguar!*

She groped around the room until she found a heavy book. A stick would have been better, but this would have to do.

In the corner of the room, she saw it: the red glow of the jaguar's eyes trained right at her.

She screamed and threw the book. The eyes merely blinked and inched closer. The jaguar growled soft and low, preparing to pounce. "No!" Amy screamed. She threw herself at the jaguar, attacking it before it could attack her. She reached for its neck, gripping it with her superstrong hands, shaking its head, hoping to keep its razor-sharp teeth from tearing her to shreds.

Then a bright light blinded her and another creature pounced on her, yanking at her arms, pulling her away from the jaguar.

"Stop it! Stop it!" she yelled. "Can't you see it's trying to kill me?"

"Amy! Amy, let go!"

Dan was yanking on her arms, trying to pull them off the jaguar's neck. But . . . it wasn't a jaguar.

It was Jake. She had her hands around his neck. He towered over her, firmly pushing her away, but she was too strong for him now. He grimaced, his eyes wide with terror. She relaxed her grip and collapsed in his arms. "Jake?" This was so confusing. What had happened to the jaguar? Jake led her to her bed. She blinked and rubbed her aching head, while he gingerly touched his sore neck. Dan sat beside her.

"What were you doing, Amy?" Dan asked. "It looked like you were trying to kill him!"

"No . . . no . . ." Dan had switched on the light. The darkness was gone. She could see clearly now. There was no jaguar, no fire. She wasn't hot anymore, though she was still drenched in sweat. In fact, in spite of the jungle heat, she was beginning to feel chilled.

"Jake, are you all right?" she asked.

"Yeah, I'm okay." Jake rubbed his neck and tried to smile, but it was strained.

"I'm sorry. I didn't mean to hurt you, I swear. But I thought—" She paused, knowing how crazy it would sound.

"Amy, tell me." Dan was pressing her hand. "What just happened to you?"

"I'm not sure," Amy said. "I thought a jaguar was in the room, attacking me."

"I heard you shouting," Jake explained. "So I came in to see if you were all right, and you leaped at me and—" He didn't finish.

"Basically tried to strangle him," Dan said.

Amy began to shake. She'd been hot only a few minutes before, but now she was freezing. "I could swear I heard growling. I saw the cat's glowing eyes right over there." She pointed at the corner by the door.

"Maybe you were dreaming," Dan suggested.

"Or hallucinating," Jake added.

Hallucinating. Oh, no. Amy tried to clear her mind, but it was still foggy. Her room had been on fire, she'd been sure of it. But then, no, it wasn't a fire, it was a jaguar . . . a jaguar had attacked her. It had seemed so real. . . .

She huddled under the covers, shivering. Her worst fear had come true. It had been nagging at her, this fear, all day, but she wanted so badly to deny it. She was suffering from the side effects.

The serum was affecting her mind. She couldn't trust herself. She was losing control of her muscles, her emotions, and her brain was misfiring, too. Her judgment was suspect. If she was capable of mistaking Jake for a jaguar, what other mistakes might she make?

Dan and Jake were watching her, concern etched on their faces. She felt a sudden rush of affection so intense it made her chest throb.

She had to make a decision now, a decision that was best for all of them. She knew what she had to do. "Dan." She put her hand over his. "I need to talk to you alone."

Jake left, shutting the door quietly behind him. Dan sat beside her on the bed, his whole body stiff with worry. "Dan," Amy said. "I need your help."

He nodded, still waiting.

"I know I'm asking a lot of you, something very big. I know you want out as soon as we're finished with Pierce. But I need you now. . . . If we don't find the antidote in time and something should happen to me, you'll be the one . . . I mean, you'll have to . . ."

Dan shook his head. "That's not going to happen, Amy. I won't let it. We're going to find the antidote in time, I promise."

Tears sprang to her eyes and dropped down her cheeks. She wanted to believe him so badly. But she knew how much they were up against. "What I'm saying is, I need you to take charge of the mission. Now." Dan bit his lip. "I know you don't want to do it," she said. "But—" She was surprised at how hard it was to ask for help at last, after refusing it all this time. It took all her strength to admit to weakness. "The serum is acting on me. You saw what just happened."

"Amy, that wasn't you."

"Exactly. I'm under the influence of the serum. I can't trust myself. And you shouldn't trust me, either."

"What are you talking about?" His eyes darted

around the room, not meeting hers. He knew where this conversation was headed.

"I'd like to think . . . I'd like to believe that, in spite of everything, if I needed you—really needed you, the way I do now—you could step in and do whatever needs to be done."

That phrase hung in the air, full of questions, full of terror: *whatever needs to be done.* "Sure, of course, Amy," he said too quickly. "You know I'll do whatever you need. Just tell me what you want me to do and—"

"Listen." She took his wrists in her two hands and shook them, trying to reach him. They'd been out of touch with each other, in a way, for weeks. She had to get through to him now. "I've taken on a lot of our responsibility myself. I know you think it's because I don't trust you to handle it. But that isn't true, Dan. I've been trying to spare you from pressure, and from danger. But I know you're smart, and strong, and capable. You can make the big decisions. You can lead the family."

As he allowed himself to hear what she was asking of him, his jittery face hardened. He looked older almost instantly, and calmer, and sadder. "I have faith in you," Amy said

Dan watched her. His hands were shaking. There was a heaviness around his eyes and mouth that no thirteen-year-old should have. It broke her heart. He pulled his wrists out of her grip and put his hands on top of hers. They were steady now. "You can count on me."

CHAPTER 18

Trilon Laboratories
Delaware

When five o'clock finally came, Nellie hung out, "working late" until everyone was gone and it was time for her real work to begin.

Nellie wished she could be in Guatemala with Amy, but she had a job to do here. Amy needed an antidote to the serum more than ever. What did Pierce do to offset the side effects of the serum? Maybe that information could ease Amy's symptoms and buy her some time. Nellie was going to find Sammy and put him to work on it—now.

Nellie's time at Trilon hadn't been a complete waste. For one thing, she'd seen the biochemists in her lab using nanotechnology to study the interactions of different compounds at the molecular level. They had a laser that could carve tiny marks on a piece of metal or glass—say, a slide they might use under a microscope. Nellie had watched them use that laser without really knowing what it was for. But she had a use for it now.

It took a few tries to get the hang of it, but she managed to carve a message onto a glass slide. The message was invisible to the naked eye but perfectly legible under a microscope. She wrapped the glass in paper to protect it from scratches and slipped it into her pocket.

She sneaked upstairs, dodging security cameras, and walked down a dark corridor until she came to the vending machine. She used her stolen ID to open the machine and sneak into the secret basement. She opened the door from the stairwell and peered into the hall.

Sammy was being led into a room—from what Nellie could see, it looked like another lab, even more high-tech than his last one—by an armed guard. The guard shoved Sammy into the room and locked the door. Then he stood outside the door, automatic weapon at the ready, guarding it.

Oh, Sammy. What had he done to earn a round-the-clock armed guard? How was Nellie ever going to get past that guy? She let the fire door shut and looked around for an alternative way in. She stood in the stairwell, empty except for a fire extinguisher hanging on the wall. And just above the fire extinguisher . . . a grate. A grate that probably led to an air vent, which you'd need if you didn't want to suffocate way down here in an underground subbasement.

The bottom of the vent was out of Nellie's reach, but if she stood on the nearest step, her fingers could just touch the screen. Maybe if she stood on the fire extinguisher . . . She took down the metal canister, set it on the bottom step, and stood on it. The canister held her weight but rolled precariously under her toes. She pulled her trusty penknife out of her pocket and unscrewed the screen from the air vent.

Wait . . . She thought she heard a noise in the hall-way on the other side of the fire door. She froze. Was someone coming?

Another noise. She quickly jumped down, replaced the fire extinguisher, and dashed up a flight of stairs. She'd just reached the second landing when she heard the subbasement door bang open. She froze again, praying that whoever was there—most likely the armed guard—wouldn't come up the stairs or notice the loose screws in the air vent.

After a few tense seconds, the door banged shut. She peeked over the railing down into the stairwell. No sign of the guard.

She tiptoed back down the stairs. All clear. She set the fire extinguisher back on the stair, stepped on it, and continued working on the screws.

She loosened the bottom two screws and dropped them into the pocket of her white lab coat. She slipped her fingers under the grate and gripped the edge of the vent. If she could just haul herself up somehow . . . But it was too high.

Then she noticed the bracket in the wall that was meant to hold the fire extinguisher. She clung to the vent with her fingers and hopped up, stepping on the bracket with her right foot to boost herself into the vent.

As she made the leap, the fire extinguisher rolled out from under her foot and fell off the step with a clatter. She scrambled up into the vent. The grate closed after her just as the door burst open. Nellie crawled back into the vent, away from the grate, just far enough to see the armed guard look around, pick up the fallen fire extinguisher, and run up the stairs to look for intruders. Another guard came out when the first one returned to the bottom landing.

"Find anything?" the second guard asked.

"No." The first guard put the fire extinguisher back on the bracket, which had been loosened slightly by Nellie's foot. "Guess it was just the fire extinguisher falling."

"That bracket needs to be tightened," the other guard said.

They stood quietly for a moment, guns at the ready, listening for any sound. Nellie held her breath.

"All clear," the first guard said. They opened the door and went back to patrolling the lab. Nellie let out her breath. *Good of those guards to care so much about fire safety.* She started crawling through the vent, searching for Sammy. Every few yards, she came to a grate. The first one looked out on the short hallway. The second onto a room that looked like an office. The third opened onto a lab. There was a bank of computers, a machine Nellie didn't recognize that flashed a white light every five seconds, a large freezer, and a lab table covered with vials, flasks, beakers, and high-powered microscopes.

From her vantage point near the ceiling, she looked down at a slim young man in a white lab coat, his face pressed to the eyepiece of a microscope, still hard at work at nine o'clock in the evening. She'd know that mop of curly black hair anywhere. Sammy.

She was about to whisper *Pssst! Sammy!* when she noticed a movement in the corner of the room. A guard sat in a chair by the freezer, while another blocked the door. Both were armed with automatic rifles.

Sammy lifted his head and wrote something in a notebook.

The fan clicked on and cool air began to flow through the vent. Nellie shivered. She was chilled and felt like she was going to sneeze.

Oh, no. NO.

She was not going to be captured because her nose tickled. That was not happening.

The inside of her nostrils tingled. She clamped her mouth shut and pinched her nose. She closed her eyes and prayed. *No, no, I will not sneeze, I will not—*

Uh-oh. It was coming. She felt the pressure from inside her lungs, the rush of air. That tickle wanted out, and she couldn't stop it. She released her nose and slowly, slowly, silently pulled in a little air. *Calm*, she told herself. *Calm. Stay calm, nose.*

She waited. The sneeze passed.

Forty-five minutes later, and still the guards watched, and still Sammy worked. He was so brave, she thought. She could have gotten him out of there, but he wouldn't leave. He stayed to help the cause.

Nellie's heart swelled for him. But her legs were cramped from sitting perfectly still in the air vent. She sent a silent ESP message to the guards: *Let the poor guy go to bed. He's got to sleep sometime.*

At last the lab door opened. The guards escorted Sammy out. They turned off the light and left.

After ten minutes, she thought it might be safe to slip down into the lab and leave him her message.

The lab was dark except for a blue security light. Nellie knocked out a slat of the grate, then reached through the hole to unscrew the screen. She climbed down into the lab, took the slide out of her pocket, and left it under Sammy's microscope.

SAMMY, AMY TOOK SERUM, FULL DOSE. ANYTHING TO DELAY THE SYMPTOMS? — N.

Then she crawled back up into the vent, using a chair to reach it. The grate shut behind her but was still loose at the bottom, so she could come and go as needed. Or maybe, when the time came — if the guards ever left him alone — Sammy would find a moment to use the vent and escape.

Don't give up, Sammy, she thought. *Amy needs you. We all need you.*

CHAPTER 19

Tikal, Guatemala

"Oh, my gosh. Look at this."

Dan watched Amy double-check to make sure she'd read the e-mail right. She'd logged onto the fake account she'd set up for practical things, like making reservations at their hotel in Tikal, just to be sure she wasn't missing any messages.

"Someone found Olivia's book," Amy told the others. "At least, he says he has. And he wants five thousand dollars to give it back."

"Who is it?" Dan leaned over her shoulder to read the message:

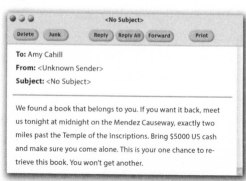

```
● ● ●                    <No Subject>
Delete   Junk        Reply  Reply All  Forward        Print

To: Amy Cahill
From: <Unknown Sender>
Subject: <No Subject>

We found a book that belongs to you. If you want it back, meet
us tonight at midnight on the Mendez Causeway, exactly two
miles past the Temple of the Inscriptions. Bring $5000 US cash
and make sure you come alone. This is your one chance to re-
trieve this book. You won't get another.
```

"It's not signed," Amy said. "And I don't recognize the e-mail address, but it's Guatemalan."

"It's got to be a trap," Jake said.

"Agreed," Dan said. "But it doesn't matter. Trap or not, we need that book."

The grim reason why they needed the book hung like a shroud over the room.

Dan pulled up a satellite map of the park and pinpointed the location for the drop. "Look at that." He pointed to a cluster of tents in the jungle, a large truck, and, not far away, an area cleared of trees. "Looks like an illegal logging camp to me. Or poachers."

Amy shook her head. "Poachers wouldn't know what the book was if they found it. Someone is using them as a cover."

"Either way," Dan said. "We've got to find the riven crystal, and we need to get Olivia's book back. Tonight."

"The four of us can't handle all that alone," Jake said. "And besides, who knows how many men have been paid to kill us this time."

"Let's bring the other guys down for backup," Dan suggested.

"No," Amy said firmly. "Why put more lives at stake than we need to?"

"Because *our* lives are at stake now," Dan insisted. "Especially yours. Amy, we need help here." He paused, suddenly feeling unsure. Amy had asked him to take charge. Now that he was doing it, was she going to stand in his way? What would he do if she did?

They stood face-to-face, each waiting for the other to back down. "Amy, it's my decision." He paused, swallowed, and worked up his courage. "And it's final."

She backed off almost too easily. "I'm sorry, Dan. I'm not used to this." He felt so sad for her now that he almost relented. The little brother in him wanted to cry out, *I take it back, Amy! I was kidding. You're in charge again, really. . . .* And he would have given anything to let her take over, if it would undo the serum, undo her death sentence, and let her live.

She smiled at him, a proud-sister smile that simultaneously annoyed and touched him. "All right. Call Ian."

At the mention of the name *Ian,* Jake flinched. She started to say something to explain, to help him understand, but he cut her off. "We need all the help we can get," he said. "I get it."

Dan hoped Amy was glad that Jake had returned to his usual gruff self and stopped fussing over her. As if things were normal. At least they were being civil to each other. It was hard to get anything accomplished when they were at each other's throats—*literally.* He dialed Attleboro on their secure line. Ian picked up. "Ian, this is Dan. We've got a lot of news to update you on."

"Dan?" Ian sounded slightly confused. "Where's Amy?"

"She's here," Dan said. "But we've had some trouble, and I'm in charge now." He glanced at Amy as he spoke. She was looking down at her lap, hands twitching slightly. Then she lifted her head and nodded at him as if to say, *That's right.*

Ian put Jonah and Hamilton on speaker for the update. Dan filled them in on the book and the blackmailers.

"The book is safe!" Ian cried. "Thank goodness. I'll gather the crew and we'll fly down immediately. Do you need anything from home?"

"Yeah," Dan said. "Bring five thousand dollars in cash. We don't think this is really about money, but that's what the blackmailers asked for."

"Will do."

"Bring Pony, too," Dan said. "We'll need everybody we can get."

"Right. Of course, you realize that after eight hours stuck on a plane with Hamilton, Jonah, and Pony, I will be a stark raving lunatic."

"You're already a stark raving lunatic," Dan teased. "Just get your butts down here."

"On our way."

"Wait." Dan looked at Amy again and blinked back the tears that sprang to his eyes. "There's one more thing you should know." There was silence over the line as Ian waited for the news, as if he sensed it was something serious. "Amy took the serum," Dan said quietly. "A full dose, undiluted. She's doing better today, but she's having some severe side effects, so—"

There was a long pause. "That's why you're in charge now," Ian said.

"Yeah."

"Oh, no," Ian whispered. "Amy. I—" Dan heard the strain in his voice as he trailed off. Ian might be lightning quick with insults and retorts, but expressing shock and sorrow didn't come so easily to him. "How long does she have?"

Dan hated to say it out loud, especially in front of Amy. But there was no way around it, and they didn't have time for anything but the truth. "About four days."

"We'll see you tonight."

A pall fell over the hotel room. Amy's leg shook restlessly. Dan felt as if someone had tied weights to his wrists and ankles, as if the smallest movement took a superhuman effort. He was responsible now for everything that happened from that moment on. It weighed on him. He could feel the responsibility pressing on his shoulders and spine like a backpack full of rocks. A lot of this was his fault. Amy had taken the serum to save him after all.

"Amy? You okay?" Dan asked.

She looked at him, her eyes hollow. "Don't worry about me. Let's just get this done."

They had until dark to make a plan. "We'll split into two groups," Dan said. "One group will go find the crystal, and the other will get the book."

"No," Amy protested. "The book pickup is a trap. It's dangerous. I'll go alone."

"Great plan, Amy," Jake countered. "You go alone, Pierce gets you *and* the book."

"Pierce doesn't know I've taken the serum," Amy said. "His men won't be expecting a girl with super-strength. I'll take them by surprise."

"You're not strong enough to take on his army alone," Dan said. "Jake is right. I'm going with you."

"And so am I," Jake said.

"No," Dan insisted. "Amy and I will handle it alone." Jake began to rise in protest, but Dan cut him off. "Period."

Jake shook his head ruefully. "You're more like your sister than you realize, Dan."

Was that true? Dan didn't know. *Remains to be seen*, he thought. "By tomorrow morning, we'll have both the crystal and the book—and we'll be that much closer to the antidote."

"That's right," Atticus said. "Nothing can stop us now, Amy."

Amy tried to smile. Dan hoped Att was right. But they'd been this close to victory so many times before, and it always seemed to slip away again, just beyond their reach.

Not this time, he vowed. *This time everything will go our way.*

For once, it has to.

CHAPTER 20

Off the coast of Maine

A tall, burnished, brawny man stood in front of J. Rutherford Pierce, squirming. Pierce himself was desperately willing his left leg to stop shaking. He rested a hand on his knee to keep the leg from kicking out involuntarily. He wondered if this man standing before him, who gleamed with strength and health, was experiencing any of the symptoms Pierce was having. After all, Pierce was responsible for enhancing the man's strength. This was Morrow, the new chief of Pierce's henchmen. Pierce had been giving them daily doses of serum for weeks now. Perhaps Morrow was squirming because he, like Pierce, was having increasingly uncontrollable spasms in his arms and legs.

Or maybe he was squirming because he was in trouble.

Pierce had sent Morrow and his men to sabotage the Cahill kids in the Guatemalan jungle. Eight grown men, made superstrong, superfast, and supersmart by the serum, attacked four normal children, and didn't manage to capture or kill a single one of them.

"That is not acceptable," Pierce said.

"I know, sir."

"You know what happened to your predecessor."

"I do, sir."

The previous chief of security and his men had been given a slow-acting poison before being sent to Tunis to capture the Cahills. Had they been successful, Pierce would have given them the antidote to the poison. They had not been successful.

Their deaths were slow and painful.

Pierce tapped his chin, pondering the best way to punish this new wayward squadron of thugs, when Morrow set a briefcase on a chair and proceeded to open it and produce something in a plastic bag.

"I know that nothing can make up for our failure," Morrow said. "But I hope this will help."

Pierce took the bag and opened it. "What is it?"

"The boy dropped it in the jungle. I'm not sure what it is, but it looks important."

It was a book—a very old book. Indeed, it was important. Very important.

"Thank you, Morrow. Good work. You are dismissed." *Please leave*, Pierce thought, glaring at Morrow. *Please get out of here so my left leg can jerk in peace.*

It was a terrible, embarrassing thought. Pierce would never let on to anyone that he had any weakness whatsoever. Still, the spasms were getting progressively worse. It was getting harder and harder for him to appear in public — and if he was going to be out on the campaign trail every day, he would need to get these symptoms under control. But how to do that without decreasing his dose of the serum?

Pierce turned his attention to the book. *Olivia Cahill's Household Book.* Some of it seemed trivial — recipes, grocery lists, chores — and some he didn't understand. There were charts, diagrams, drawings, and pages written in languages he didn't know.

Then he found a section that prickled the neatly trimmed silver hair on the back of his neck: *Perdites Civitates Codex.* He didn't know exactly what it was, but he recognized the places the Cahill kids had been to recently: Troy, Carthage, Tikal . . . and Angkor. That must be where they were headed next.

He'd go to Cambodia himself and beat them to whatever it was they were looking for. They seemed to be gathering rare ingredients: the whiskers of an Anatolian leopard, silphium, chips of riven crystal, and — aha — snake venom from Angkor Wat. But why? What were they up to?

The answer became clear as he studied Olivia's book more closely. Some of these "recipes" were more complicated than they looked. Olivia seemed to be working out ways to counteract the effects of the serum her husband had invented.

Then Pierce understood. Olivia Cahill had formulated an antidote to the serum. And Amy and Dan were gathering the ingredients to make it.

They were trying to take his power away from him. He must not allow that to happen. His bid to take over the world would be a failure.

J. Rutherford Pierce did not tolerate failure.

His men had let him down so far. But the kids wouldn't be able to fight them off forever. The Pierce army would fulfill its mission; the Cahills would die. And now it was more urgent than ever. But as he was thinking these grim thoughts, another realization began to dawn on him. He had recruited his brilliant friend Dr. Jeffrey Callender to dilute the serum, to find a way to make the side effects more tolerable. Dr. Callender and his team were working night and day on this project, but they hadn't come up with a solution yet. *Maybe*, Pierce thought, *the solution is right here in this book.* If his own labs could produce the antidote, it might be used to offset the effects of the serum.

He would be able to take the serum forever — without muscle spasms or any bad effects at all.

He could be unstoppable.

CHAPTER 21

Trilon Laboratories
Delaware

Nellie sat at her desk, trying to look busy while a worker glued a label to her door:

NADINE GORMEY

VICE PRESIDENT, BIOCHEMICAL RESEARCH

Hilarious. She—Nellie Gomez—was posing as someone who knew thing one about biochemistry—enough to boss around a staff of PhD chemists—and getting away with it. She would have had a good laugh about the whole thing if it wasn't so serious.

Had Sammy found the message she'd left on his microscope? Was he okay? And had he figured out how to slow Amy's symptoms? She hoped he'd find a way to get word back to her, somehow.

Dr. Stevens's assistant had sent her a memo entitled "Password for Access to Classified Files, Level 3," with a password and instructions for logging into a top secret file-sharing system.

Interesting. So there was a top secret file-sharing system, and now that she was a vice president, she had access to it. *Why just Level 3, though?* That meant there was a Level 2 and a Level 1. And Nellie had a feeling that Level 1 was where she'd find the good stuff.

She logged into Level 3 and looked around. Not much there she didn't already know: They were ordered to work on reducing the side effects of a certain drug, but no one really knew exactly what that drug was. The names, contact info, and backgrounds of the chemists who worked under her were listed, but no mention of Sammy by name.

She forwarded the memo to Pony, asking him to hack into Level 1 and get back to her. She went to the coffee station for a refill, and by the time she got back to her desk, Pony had cracked it.

Use this password to log into Level 1, he wrote, sending her a series of numbers.

Thanks, she wrote back. *Any news from Attleboro?*

Yeah—we're all on the Wizardmobile, flying down to Tikal. I'm set. Jonah's got a fridge stocked with Electroshock Caffeine Blast in every flavor, including ones I didn't know they made. Jalapeño Chocolate!

Good, Nellie wrote, but she was frustrated. Amy had four days left to live. Nellie wanted to be there, too. Instead she was stuck in this sterile corporate lab . . . *doing crucial work*, she reminded herself. Work that needed to be done to save her girl.

Using Pony's password, she logged into the

Classified File System, Level 1. Now *this* was interesting. There were memos and research reports from various scientists she didn't recognize. There were a few bogus reports she *did* recognize. She'd managed to fake the atomic structure of some compound she'd never heard of by drawing the shape of her favorite Putt-Putt golf course. That was a highlight.

There was a lot of chatter about one particular researcher: a certain SM.

Sammy Mourad?

He was never mentioned by name, but the more she read, the more Nellie was convinced that this was Sammy. He reported on his findings, giving them a few tidbits — *I've found something close to the molecular structure we're looking for, just one molecule away. . . .* Even Nellie could tell it was bogus. He was stalling for time.

She wished he'd find a way to get a message back to her. She couldn't take this waiting any longer. She had to *do* something.

Fiske, Nellie thought. He might know something about the serum that she could use, something that could buy some time for Amy.

She called his room at the Callender Institute. A nurse answered and said that Mr. Cahill was in therapy and couldn't come to the phone.

Therapy my toenails, Nellie thought. She left her office, got into her car, and drove straight up to New York.

CHAPTER 22

Tikal, Guatemala

Dan loved burritos, but every time he tried to take a bite his stomach clenched in protest. He was in a rare state: so nervous he could hardly eat.

Ian, Ham, Jonah, and Pony had arrived, and they'd all met for an early dinner to plan that night's missions. They had two goals: to get the riven crystal and to meet with the blackmailers to get Olivia's book.

It was going to be a big night.

Ian, Ham, Jonah, and Pony seemed uncomfortable, too, at first. Ian kept glancing at the bruises on Jake's neck, but for once was too shaken to comment. Jonah tried to act as if nothing was wrong. "What up," he said casually, giving a solemn nod to Dan. He enveloped Amy in a bear hug and held her a second longer than usual, but he couldn't quite meet her eye, as if he didn't know what to say to her.

And on greeting Amy, who was still glowing as if she'd been trapped in a nuclear reactor, Ham was so surprised he blurted out, "Amy, you look amazing! You don't look like you're going to—" A kick to the shin from Jonah shut him up before he could finish that morbid sentence. But everyone caught the anguished look on Amy's face.

Pony shifted nervously, staring at his neon green sneakers. But as soon as he saw Amy he said, "Whatever I can do to help, just tell me. Anything you need." He touched the top of his hairline with his index finger in a kind of chivalrous gesture of respect—at least, that was what Dan guessed he was going for—before getting fascinated with his sneakers again.

Dan got them down to business. Everyone agreed that the only way to accomplish everything in one night was to split into two groups. What they didn't agree on was who should go where.

"Ham, Jonah, Atticus, Jake, Pony, and Ian," Dan said. "You go after the crystal. We've got a map to lead you there. You'll leave just after sundown." Jake threw Ian a wary glance. Dan knew he didn't want to be grouped with Ian, but they'd just have to set their personal gripes aside for now.

"Whoa, wait a minute," Jonah said. "Who's going with you and Amy?"

"You're walking into a trap," Ian said. "It's a suicide mission."

"What choice do we have?" Dan said. "Without the book—" *Without the book, Amy dies*, he thought, but he couldn't say it out loud.

"Fine," Jonah said. "But you'll need backup."

"I appreciate the offer," Dan said. "But I can't let any of you do that for us. It's too big a sacrifice."

"What?!" Ham protested. "This is our fight, too."

"Ian said it himself: It's a suicide mission." Dan glanced at Amy, who looked sad. He was beginning to understand the reasoning behind so many of her earlier decisions, the ones that had infuriated him, the ones where she'd abandoned him so she could go off and fight alone. "I can't ask that of any of you."

"But I volunteer!" Ham jumped to his feet.

"So do I!" Jonah said.

"And I," Ian added.

Jake and Atticus stood with them. Their voices rang out in the silence of the room. Pony looked around uncomfortably. Every boy was on his feet except for him. So he rose. "Me too."

Amy blinked back tears. "You all have other jobs to do."

"The blackmailers told us to come alone," Dan said. "If they spot you, it could make things worse."

"I can stay here and monitor communications with them," Pony said. "I mean, you know, I volunteer to—"

"Thanks, Pony," Amy said. "That's the perfect job for you. If we get into trouble, you can call the others. Dan and I will be okay on our own," she continued. "We need all five of you to stay together. You could be sabotaged on your way to the temple, just like last time."

Jake turned to Dan. "And you're going along with this?"

Dan pushed his plate away untouched. He was in charge now, and that made him so tense he lost his appetite once and for all.

"Amy and I discussed it, and we agree," Dan said. "You guys need each other for protection. With her power, the two of us should be okay on our own."

"Possibly," Ian said. "But you don't know that for sure. In fact, you don't know what you're getting into at all."

"Pony will be monitoring the lines of communication for signs of trouble," Amy said. "We'll be okay—I promise." None of the others looked satisfied with her word, but Dan sensed that they hesitated to challenge her as vigorously as they normally would. They didn't know how to behave around someone who was dying.

"We need that crystal," Dan told the others. "I want the five of you to go into the jungle and find it tonight. And come back safely. Period." Dan heard himself speak the words—giving orders to five boys who were older than he was—but it didn't feel real. He felt as if he were watching himself take charge from outside his own body. Watching some other boy, some boy who looked exactly like him but who had way more confidence than the real Dan would ever have.

But, to his surprise, everyone listened. He may have been faking it, but he was faking it real enough to make it work.

CHAPTER 23

The Callender Institute
New York City

Nellie found Fiske propped up in bed in a hospital gown. There was a new tension in the air at the Callender Institute. For one thing, the staff had changed, and some of the health care workers she'd passed in the hall looked awfully buff for nurses. When she opened the door to Fiske's room, his eyes widened in fear. He relaxed when he saw it was her. But she didn't like that first look on his face. What usually happened when the door to his room opened?

"Fiske, how are you doing?" She moved a chair next to the bed.

Fiske licked his lips. "Nellie, thank goodness . . ." His mouth seemed dry. He had trouble speaking.

"Want some water?" Nellie had brought some gourmet treats for him, but he didn't seem capable of eating, let alone enjoying them. She poured water into a paper cup. His hands shook so badly he could hardly hold it. "Here, let me help you."

She held the cup while he took a few sips. She had never seen him so weak. He wasn't getting better at all. He was getting worse. "Fiske, I need to talk to you," she said. "I need you to tell me anything you know about the serum. Anything at all . . ."

Fiske stared at the wall. Was he listening? Nellie followed his eyes, trying to figure out what was so fascinating. She couldn't see anything on the wall besides a painting of a seascape.

"It's a matter of life and death," Nellie went on. "You see, Amy —"

He wasn't listening, she was sure of it. He gaped at the wall in horror, unable to tear his eyes away. "Fiske? What is it?"

He didn't answer, but he got that frightened look again. "Fiske?"

"There's a portal. Do you see it?" He pointed a shaky finger at the wall, which looked completely solid to Nellie. "A hole has opened up right there, leading to another dimension. . . ."

Nellie went to the wall, touched it, knocked on it. "I don't see anything. No portal, Fiske."

"Grace! For heaven's sake, Grace, get away from that portal!"

Nellie ran back to Fiske's side. "I'm not Grace. I'm Nellie."

"Shh! Hide, Grace. They'll hear you!"

He's hallucinating, Nellie realized.

"Wait!" He leaned away from her. "You're not Grace!"

Good—he was coming back to his senses. "That's right, Fiske. I'm—"

"I know who you are," Fiske hissed. "You're out to get me, aren't you? You're trying to kill me!"

"Fiske, no, I'm Nellie! I'm trying to help you!"

"Nurse! Nurse!" Fiske hit the call button and one of the buff nurses burst into the room.

"Is everything okay in here?"

Fiske didn't answer. He was shaking and confused. "Everything's fine," Nellie said. "He got a little worked up over a joke I told him, but he's okay now."

"He looks worn out. Visiting hours are over." The nurse pulled Nellie to her feet and pushed her firmly to the door.

Nellie pushed back. "Wait, please. Just give me a few more minutes with him. Just a few more minutes."

The nurse's biceps bulged as she crossed her brawny arms over her chest and frowned. "Five minutes. Then you're out of here."

Nellie shut the door firmly behind the departing nurse. What was going on here? The Callender Institute was revered as one of the best hospitals in the world. And yet . . . Fiske's symptoms struck Nellie as eerily familiar: tremors, visions, paranoia, extreme mood swings. . . .

The serum.

Was Fiske taking the serum? Or was it being given

to him? And if he was, how did the hospital get their hands on it? It didn't matter, Nellie decided. The main thing was to get Fiske out of there before he was poisoned to death.

She sat on the bed next to Fiske, who had calmed down a bit. She gave him more water. "Feeling better?"

He nodded.

"Fiske, I think they're testing the serum on you." She didn't finish the rest of that thought—that the serum was killing him—and killing Amy, too. "I've got to get you out of here. Can we check you out? I'll drive you to Attleboro or take you somewhere else where you'll be well cared for. The main thing is you can't stay here."

"Yes," he rasped in a hoarse voice. "I want to leave."

"Good. I'll talk to Dr. Callender and arrange it. I'll be back in ten minutes." Nellie hurried through the busy halls. There were cameras every few feet, and more nurses' stations than most hospitals had. *Nurses' stations or security stations?*

She found Dr. Callender's office. His secretary stopped her from going in, saying he was on the phone. Nellie waited, and a few minutes later the secretary said she could see him. The doctor smiled when Nellie walked in. "Ms. Gomez. To what do I owe the pleasure?"

"I've just been to see Fiske Cahill and . . . he told me he'd like to check out of here. Today."

Dr. Callender's smile faded slightly and he touched the tips of his fingers together. "I see. Well, I'm afraid that isn't possible."

"It isn't? He's here voluntarily, isn't he?"

"Yes, he was admitted voluntarily, and normally he'd be allowed to come and go as he pleased."

"So what is the problem?"

"You say you've just been to see him. How did he seem to you?"

"Well . . ." Nellie hesitated. If she admitted that he seemed very sick to her, that would weaken her case for dismissal. "He seemed fine. The main point is, he wants to leave. So if you'll just give me the papers to sign or whatever we have to do—"

"Mr. Cahill cannot leave. I'm sorry." Dr. Callender's grin was wide and wolfish now, and Nellie's pulse began to race. She sensed danger but wasn't sure why.

"He can and he will. I'm taking him out of here right now, and you can't stop me."

"Ms. Gomez, Mr. Cahill is not mentally competent. Legally, I must hold him here if I deem him a danger to himself or others, and he is certainly a danger to himself, at the very least."

It seemed impossible for that wolfish grin to grow wider, and yet it did. Nellie shivered. "He's perfectly fine," she insisted. "I want a second opinion."

"You're welcome to it. Any doctor who examines him would come to the same conclusion."

He's right, Nellie thought bitterly. Fiske was hallucinating—because they were drugging him. Her eyes fell on a paper in Dr. Callender's inbox. A report on the results of some drug research—from

Dr. Huang at Trilon Labs. Nellie's skin prickled. Suddenly she knew.

He was in on it. In on the whole thing.

She couldn't breathe.

"And now, Ms. Gomez, if you would kindly leave?" Dr. Callender said. "Or would you like me to have one of the nurses escort you out?"

She was trembling, but tried to hide it. She couldn't trust anyone. Not even a famous doctor. She felt as if a noose were tightening around her neck. Fiske was being held prisoner, and poisoned in the name of research. Amy was four days away from death. And Dr. Callender was working for Pierce.

Dr. Callender pressed a button. "Marco, will you please show Ms. Gomez out?"

The door opened and a burly bald man in a security uniform stepped inside.

"That won't be necessary." Nellie slipped past the man and out the door. "I can find the way myself."

She shook the whole drive back to Delaware. She had to find a way to spring Fiske from Dr. Callender's Hospital of Death.

That would have made a good name for a punk band if it weren't so real.

If only Sammy were free, he could help her. But his work at the lab was too important. He was her only hope now.

She went into her office and checked her Level 1 account. Someone had sent her a recipe for chicken tagine. Weird. Who at this place even knew she liked to cook?

Sammy, that's who.

The recipe was a coded message. It had to be, because any dish that called for a cup of salt was not going to taste good.

Nellie set to work decoding the message. She recognized the recipe from her favorite Moroccan cookbook. She found the recipe online. It didn't call for a cup of salt, of course—it called for a teaspoon. There were forty-eight teaspoons in a cup of salt. Maybe this was a simple alphabet code. Nellie hoped so—coding was so not her strong point. She counted forty-eight characters from the numeral 1 in "1 cup of salt" and landed on a G. So maybe G equaled A? She tried decoding the message but it didn't quite work.

Come on, Sammy. Don't make this too hard for me.

But she knew he couldn't make it too easy—or too obvious—or he would get caught.

Then she noticed that Sammy's recipe called for two cups of butter—truly insane—and that the real recipe called for two tablespoons.

Aha.

There were sixteen tablespoons in a cup. Maybe the sixteenth letter was the equivalent for letter number 2, B?

Yes. Working through a few more kinks like that—three pounds of couscous gave her the equivalent for C—Nellie managed to decode Sammy's message:

```
Pierce knows about the antidote. He
wants to use it to make a less lethal
version of the serum. Forced me to
switch gears and work on combining
antidote and serum. If he succeeds,
Amy's antidote will not work on Pierce's
serum. We will have no way to stop him.
We will be powerless.

Will try to sabotage. Once that's done,
I want to blow this place. And leave
nothing behind.
```

Nellie bit her lip. How did Pierce know about the antidote? There was only one way she could think of: Olivia Cahill's book. His men must have found it when Dan lost it in the jungle.

So they were in even more trouble than they knew. Amy was dying. They still had to find the riven crystal, and they'd lost the book that would tell them how to make the antidote. And on top of all that, Pierce knew that the kiddos had found a way to stop him.

The Attleboro boys had flown down to Guatemala to help Dan and Amy get the riven crystal and the book — which they thought was being held by blackmailers. The whole thing was a trap. The book wasn't even there. And only she could warn them.

CHAPTER 24

Tikal, Guatemala

"Shhh! Wait! Lights out!"

Hamilton Holt held out his arms as a signal to freeze. Jake clicked off his flashlight. A few yards ahead, one of the park guards crossed the causeway on security patrol. He was whistling, his rifle slung over his shoulder.

Jake held his breath. He and the others—Hamilton, Atticus, Ian, and Jonah—waited without moving until the guard's whistling faded, then disappeared. Once he was out of earshot, they relaxed. "Okay," Hamilton said. "Onward."

"That guy has no idea what's going down tonight," Jonah said.

"Let's hope nothing does go down," Jake said. "Let's find the crystal and get back as soon as possible." He was anxious to find out if Amy and Dan had gotten the book back—and made it out of that trap alive. If they needed help, he wanted to be there, ready to go.

He flicked on his flashlight and shined it at the map Atticus held. Atticus was in charge of navigation — tracing the mirror image of their earlier trek to find the hidden temple that contained the riven crystal. The group had left at sundown to avoid being detected by the park guards. But the jungle seemed to be swarming with them.

"They're on high alert because of the poachers," Atticus theorized. He studied the map and then pointed down a narrow path. "That way. It's not far now."

They set out again, pushing the thick vegetation away from their faces. The night was humid and sticky, and mosquitoes buzzed in their ears. A full moon rose over the treetops, lighting their way but also lighting them up, making them more visible to the guards, or any enemies that might be waiting to pounce. Luckily, the trees made lots of shadows to hide in.

The path forked unexpectedly into two smaller trails. "Which way?" Jonah asked.

Jake looked from the map to the fork. "This way," he said, aiming his flashlight at the trail on the right.

"No, mate," Ian said. "You're reading the bloody map wrong. We're headed south — see?" He drew one well-groomed fingernail along the paper to the temple they were trying to find.

Jake was annoyed, but he tried to restrain himself. "I know how to read a 'bloody map.' And I know this park pretty well by now. You just got here. We're taking the right fork."

"Listen," Ian said through gritted teeth. "I wouldn't make a fuss if Amy's life wasn't at stake. But every second counts."

At the mention of Amy, Jake's muscles tensed. "I know Amy's life is in danger. That's why I'm here. If we hurry, we might get back in time to go after her and Dan—"

"They were told to come alone. If we show up, they could be killed."

"They're probably going to be killed anyway," Jake said. "And you're willing to stand by and let that happen?"

"I never said any such thing—"

Jonah stepped between Ian and Jake, who were glaring at each other in the dark. "Whoa, let's cool it now. We're all here for Amy. It doesn't matter who's right or wrong. All that matters is that we find this freaking crystal and get back to Dan and Amy in one piece. Hamilton, which way should we go?"

Jake sighed and let it go. Jonah was right. Normally, everything about Ian made Jake want to shove him into the messiest mud puddle he could find, just to watch him weep over his ruined designer shoes. Yet tonight, the smug expression seemed forced, more of a mask to hide what he was really feeling. He was the most arrogant person Jake had ever met, but he also cared about Amy. They all did. Maybe more than they'd admitted.

A lot more than they'd admitted to her.

Hamilton gaped at the map and shook his head. "This path winds around a lot, so it's hard to tell. . . ."

"Okay, Hamilton is stumped," Jonah said. "Atticus?"

"The right path. I'm pretty sure that's the one on the map."

"The right path it is." Jonah led the way, taking the right fork. Jake and the others followed, Ian grumbling something about brothers sticking together.

"That's right." Jonah stopped short and turned around to school Ian. "Brothers stick together. And we're all brothers in this. So we stick together. Got it?"

Ian nodded, and they continued down the path. *Tell him, Jonah*, Jake thought in silent satisfaction.

After trekking another half hour, Atticus stopped in front of a dense cluster of trees. "This is it."

Jake strained to see. From where they were standing, the temple looked like a mound of green under the moonlight, but he could just make out the ruined remains of a pyramid near the top leaves.

"This temple hasn't been excavated yet," Atticus explained. "The altar could be buried under tons of stone."

"Or some of that stone could crumble while we're digging around in there," Jonah said. "And crush us."

"We won't know until we start." Hamilton had already cleared away some vines until he found a round stone hole. He ripped off more vines. The hole began to take shape in the moonlight.

"It looks like—like a mouth," Atticus said.

"A jaguar's mouth," Ian added.

"With teeth," Jonah finished.

They worked at clearing the vines away, removing fallen stones and clumps of dirt, until the hole became a long, dark tunnel. "Is that the way into the temple?" Jonah asked.

Atticus peered inside, nodding. "There are other ruins in the Tikal complex that have intimidating entrances, serpent's maws for doors, that sort of thing. But this looks pretty scary."

"Who's going to go first?" Ian asked.

"I will." Jake bent down and crawled into the tunnel, his flashlight in one hand. The others followed. Something brushed against his face. He recoiled, sat up, and hit his head on the top of the tunnel.

"Jake, what happened?" Atticus called from behind.

"Nothing. Just a spiderweb." The tunnel seemed endless. It looped and turned like a maze. Every few feet, Jake's light caught a glint of white embedded in the wall. Bones? "Att, were people buried in this temple?" he called out.

"Probably. A lot of the temples were used for burial."

"Great. Just checking." He tried not to think about the fact that he was crawling on his hands and knees through a pitch-black tunnel of bones.

The tunnel gradually grew wider, until at last Jake could stand. He stepped through what might have been a doorway or the remains of a gate and found himself under the moonlight again.

"All that crawling just to get back outside," Ian grumbled.

"The top of the temple must have caved in centuries ago," Atticus observed.

Just as Att said, the temple had four standing walls but no roof. It was like a square or a clearing with a small step pyramid at one end. The trees were so dense that the moonlight barely reached through the branches, dotting the ground with jagged bits of light like pieces of broken glass. Jake shone his flashlight on the stone monolith in front of him. The top third of the pyramid inside the temple had crumbled and one wall had rotted away, leaving the structure open on one side. In front of him stood a stela with a menacing face carved in the stone: a large nose, squinting eyes, and mouth open in a roar, as if to shout, *Keep out!*

He stepped over a pile of boulders to enter the pyramid. There was a stone floor, a row of broken stone benches, and at one end a high table that might have once been part of an altar. Cobwebs filled the corners, and a bat flitted over their heads.

"Creepy," Jonah said.

"Yes, let's not linger," Ian said. "Atticus, where do you think the altar was?"

"Here!" Atticus picked his way over the piles of rocks to the high table against the back wall. It was set into a kind of nave, with a niche carved into the wall behind it that might have held candles or sacred icons. The table was decorated with intricately carved

Mayan designs that looked familiar to Jake. Some were abstract—mazes, stars, pyramids—but others showed men in strange poses wearing large Mayan headgear.

All the boys aimed their lights at the back wall. "Look for a stone with a different color or texture than the others," Atticus told them. "Or something that might have been added on later."

Jake moved the light methodically from stone to stone, but nothing looked unusual to him. Then he trained his beam on the front of the altar table. "Hey—what's this?" He brushed away some dirt and vines. There was a large, familiar carving. His heart started racing. He'd seen this in Olivia's book, he was sure. Almost sure . . . He swept away more dirt for a clearer view. The carving showed a man wearing a large headdress with three panels. *Please be what I think this is*, he prayed. All he needed was Atticus's confirmation.

"Hey, Att—I think this is the Lord of the Mirrors."

Att hurried over to Jake. He ran his hands over the carving. Jake held his breath. "Well?"

"It is." Atticus beamed. "The riven crystal must be set somewhere in this table." Jake let out his breath in a sigh of relief. They were so close. . . .

The others ran over. They all aimed their flashlights at the table, searching for a piece of stone that looked different from the rectangular slabs of limestone. Jake found another glint, right under the Lord of the Mirrors. Set in the center of the thick table was a square stone, slightly darker than the others and smooth to the touch. "Att! I think I found the crystal!"

Atticus knelt down to examine the stone while the others crowded around. "This is it—riven quartz crystal."

"Finally!" Jake said. "Let's take what we need and get out of here."

Ian took a penknife from his pocket. "This blade should do." He grinned. "We Lucians always keep our blades sharp." With the practiced skill of a Lucian, Ian shaved off bits of stone into a box Atticus had brought.

"Make sure we get enough—at least an ounce."

"I'm working on it," Ian said. "Shaving rock isn't easy, you know."

Jake looked up to see bats fluttering through the canopy of trees. "Hurry," he urged. "We don't want to hang around here too long. You never know when we might be ambushed." He stood very still and listened for any sign of intruders. Night birds screeched and monkeys rustled through the treetops, but he heard no footsteps and saw no lights.

"You got enough?" Jonah asked. Ian nodded.

"The coast is clear," Jake said. "Let's go." They'd completed their mission: They had the crystal at last. Jake's spirits lifted as they marched back toward the hotel. They were one step—one big step—closer to saving Amy.

But then the reality hit him, how many more steps they had to go, and his mood plummeted. *Four days,* he thought. *Four days.*

CHAPTER 25

Pony was alone in the hotel, eyes and fingers glued to his laptop, when his cell rang. "Jake, what up?" Pony asked, without a trace of humor in his voice. Amy and Dan had left about twenty minutes earlier to meet the blackmailers, and Pony was tracing the ransom e-mails in search of their source. He hadn't found it yet, but he didn't like the direction the trail was headed in.

"We've got the crystal and we're on our way back," Jake reported.

"Excellent!" Pony said. "Dan and Amy left a little while ago. They're out of cell range by now, but they'll be stoked to hear this." *Now all we need is the book*, he thought, *and we're almost there.*

"We've just crossed the Mendez Causeway," Jake said. "We nearly got busted by the patrol guards, so we're lying low for a while till they move out of the area."

"Gotcha. Stay safe." Pony clicked off and went back to monitoring the blackmailers' line. He'd volunteered to stay behind and track the chatter because he was afraid of action. He could admit it to himself or to anyone who asked him. Those Pierce guys were no joke.

But Pony took the job he did have very seriously. And now that he was doing it, he felt more like part of the team than ever. Practically a Cahill. *If Dan or Amy asked me to go with them now, I'd go.* And he meant it. But he was more useful here in the hotel. No doubt about that. There'd been no electronic activity all night. Dead quiet. That made him nervous. So he tried to trace the original e-mail, see where it came from.

This should have been easy. If the blackmail message came from poachers or villagers, it would have been. But the true source of the message was strangely elusive. Following a hunch, Pony hacked into April May's e-mail.

Bingo.

He couldn't find the actual ransom note, but he did find Amy's fake e-mail address in April's contact list.

So April knew about Amy's fake account, and had had some contact with it.

Her contact list was also riddled with Pierce's addresses, his various accounts, his wife's, his kids'. . . .

He opened a file marked "P." E-mails from Pierce, including his orders to keep tabs on Amy and Dan and inform him of every move they made. Pony rubbed his eyes and shook his head. *Oh, April May, whoever you are*, he thought sadly. He was seized with an impulse to write to her, and then, just as quickly, seized with a bout of shyness.

Forget the shyness, he said to himself. Go for it.

He'd learned a lot in the short time he'd been with the Cahills, and one of the biggest lessons was not to hold back. Go for it now, because you never knew what could happen the next day, or even the next minute. So he composed a quick note:

```
Dear April May, my computer compadre,

Someday, when all this craziness is
over, I hope to meet you in person.
Like enemy soldiers meeting on neutral
ground after a truce. We can trade
notes and secrets, and who knows, we
might find out we have more in common
than just lightning fingers. . . .
— P
```

A few minutes later, his message signal dinged.

```
I'd love that, Pony. Let's work together
to end this war now. Because it is a
war.

Take care of yourself. I'm not just
saying that. Please watch out. There's
danger everywhere.

I'll keep an eye on you.
— AM
```

Pony felt a tingle rise from his toes to the tip of his ponytail. Someday . . . someday.

He caught himself daydreaming and snapped out of it. The Cahills needed him. Amy and Dan needed him — especially Amy. They'd lured him out of his parents' garage into a world that was more dangerous than he'd ever imagined. But he wasn't sorry. He'd grown to love them, all of them, even that grouchy twit Ian.

His cell buzzed. Text coming in. From Nellie.

THE BOOK'S NOT THERE. PIERCE'S MEN
WAITING. I TRIED AMY AND DAN — NO
ANSWER. DON'T LET THEM GO, PONY. STOP
THEM!

His first instinct was to panic. *What do I do? What do I do?* Dan and Amy were out of cell range. If he ran, maybe he could stop them before they reached the meeting place.

If he ran? How fast could he possibly run on his rubbery, computer-jock, pizza-and-Electroshock-fueled legs? Jake and the others were still half an hour's walk from the hotel. They wouldn't get back in time.

It had to be him.

Just in case, Pony called Amy, then Dan. The calls went straight to voice mail. No service. They were too far out in the jungle. There was only one way to reach them.

Run.

CHAPTER 26

Trilon Laboratories
Delaware

"Pssst! Sammy!"

Sammy lifted his head from his microscope. He looked around the room. He didn't see anyone. He went back to his research. He pressed his eye to the microscope, then pulled it away and wrote some figures in his notebook.

From her vantage point—the air vent over Sammy's workstation—Nellie took the luxury of one minute to admire his curly hair, how elegant and serious he looked while he worked. His smooth olive skin had gotten a little sallow from being locked up in an underground lab all this time, but he still made Nellie's heart race.

"Nellie?"

"Up here." Sure now that the coast was clear, she pushed open the air vent grate and slid into the lab. Sammy went to help ease her down.

"Careful," he whispered. "There's an armed guard right outside the door."

Nellie scanned the room. If the guard turned around to look through the window in the door, he'd see her. She ducked behind Sammy's workstation. Sammy squatted down to talk to her, but she said, "No — stay up there and pretend to keep working, in case the guard checks. He'll come in if he doesn't see you."

Sammy stood up and started to sort some slides. "I'm so sorry," he murmured. "I've been racking my brain, but I can't think of anything that will help Amy besides the antidote."

Nellie grimaced, her chest tightening under the weight of her disappointment. "It's okay. You just need more time to focus. No one can work while surrounded by these creepy guards and eating terrible food." She reached for his hand. "Now can you get out of here? I know a vent we can take."

Sammy glanced at the door. The back of the guard's head was visible. He wasn't looking — at the moment. But all he had to do was turn his head forty-five degrees and he'd see everything.

"I should stay," he said. "I can't sabotage Pierce's research unless I'm here."

"The longer you stay, the more danger you're in. You've done enough, Sammy. More than enough. And I'm going to destroy this place."

He looked down at her and sighed. She could see on his face that he could hardly stand another minute of captivity. "All right. Let's go. Quick." He pulled Nellie to her feet and boosted her up to the vent. She crawled in, then turned around and reached out to pull Sammy up. He put a chair under the vent and started scrambling up when the door burst open. Nellie dragged him into the vent and pulled the grate shut.

Had the guard noticed?

She held her breath. She was desperate to crawl away but afraid it would make too much noise.

Sammy gripped her hand. He'd just barely made it into the vent. One of his feet was pressed against the grate. That's when she noticed his shoe was untied. And the lace was dangling outside the vent.

She pointed to his foot and pantomimed, *Pull it in!*

Too late.

"Hey—what's that?" the guard asked.

"Come on, Sammy!" Nellie yanked on his arm and started crawling through the vent, but the guard had seen the shoelace. He tore the grate off the vent, jumped up on the chair, and reached inside. He grabbed Sammy's legs, yelling, "Stop!"

"Nellie! He's got me!"

Nellie turned and grabbed Sammy's arms in a tug-of-war with the guard, but the guard was too strong. He yanked Sammy out of the vent and down to the floor. Another guard had heard the shout and ran into the room just as Nellie tried to disappear the other way. He jumped up on the chair, dove into the vent, and grabbed Nellie by the feet. "Let go of me!"

She kicked him right in the face.

"Oof!" The guard grunted but didn't let go. He pulled her down through the vent opening and back into the lab. The room was full of guards now, five of them. They'd already restrained Sammy. Nellie screamed, "Five against two? Try fighting fair, creeps!"

She pulled out her best move, the three-kick special: a roundhouse kick followed by a knee to the chin, finishing with a high front kick. But five serum-enhanced thugs were too much for her. They gagged her and tied her hands behind her back. "Let's go."

The goons marched Sammy and Nellie out of the lab and down the hall to an elevator. "Just to be safe," one guard said, taking two blindfolds out of his jacket pocket. He blindfolded Sammy and then Nellie. "In case you get any clever ideas."

"There's no escape from where they're going," another guard said. Nellie heard the elevator door open. The guard forced her forward. She stumbled. She heard the door close, felt her insides rise as the elevator dropped.

Going down.

The door opened and she felt a blast of chilly air. She was marched forward a few yards. Keys jangled. A lock turned. A door opened, and she was shoved through it.

Her blindfold was lifted. She and Sammy were in a small, windowless room. A cell, really. The air vent was tiny, rat-sized. The door had no window.

The guards untied her and left, locking the door

behind them. Nellie looked at Sammy. "I'm so sorry."

Nellie knew it was hopeless, but she couldn't stop herself from trying the door. The knob didn't turn. She banged and pounded on it, desperate to get out. Sammy slammed himself against the door, hoping to break it down. The door barely vibrated. Through the thick metal, Nellie thought she heard the guards laughing.

They were trapped, with no way out. "They've got to come back," Nellie said. "How can you do their research for them if you're locked in a cell?"

Sammy's large brown eyes looked tired. "Believe me, they can do whatever they want."

She pressed her back against the wall and slid to the floor in despair. Sammy sat beside her and rested his head on her shoulder.

She couldn't get to Amy. Fiske was dying, too. And now there was nothing she could do.

That knowledge nearly killed her.

CHAPTER 27

Tikal, Guatemala

"There it is."

Amy and Dan crouched in the brush just outside the poachers' camp. The full moon was both a blessing and a curse—a blessing because it was so bright that Dan and Amy didn't need to use their flashlights, which would have given them away. And a curse because it was harder to hide from the park guards swarming the forest. But at the camp there was no sign of life, not even the smoking ashes of a campfire. Where were the blackmailers hiding?

There were definitely poachers here, or had been at some point. Loggers had cleared about an acre of mahogany trees. The wood was stacked on the back of a truck, ready to be sneaked out of the forest. Tents were set up at the far end near a crumbling temple. The poachers had ruined part of the jungle and endangered the habitat of multiple birds and animals.

On top of that, they were apparently eager to accept

Pierce's dirty money and hide his men for him. "Do you remember the instructions?" she whispered to Dan.

Dan nodded, hefting the small sack of cash. Earlier in the evening the blackmailers had e-mailed specific instructions on how and where to leave the money and find the book. "Leave the money at the foot of the temple. There will be a note on the bottom step telling us where to find the book."

"There had better be." Amy gritted her teeth. She was itching to get the book and get out of there. The nerves just under her skin prickled with electricity. She wasn't sure if that was the serum acting on her nervous system or if her sharply honed instincts for danger were trying to warn her of something.

"You give the signal," she told Dan. He nodded again, scanning the clearing carefully. They watched for any sign of movement. Behind them, the jungle teemed with nocturnal life. But in the clearing, all was still.

They had to cross the clearing to get to the temple, a crumbling, half-excavated pyramid still covered with vines. The poachers might have started excavating it, hoping to find some treasures to sell. One side of the temple looked like a simple mound of dirt, while on the other side some dirt had been dug away to reveal part of a stone step pyramid. The moon lit up the clearing like a searchlight. There was no way to cross it unnoticed, nowhere to hide. That was where they'd be most vulnerable.

Dan watched for another moment. Just as Amy was thinking there was no point in putting it off any longer, Dan tapped her on the forearm. *Go.*

Crouching, they crept out into the open. Amy braced herself for attack, but nothing happened. They were a few yards away from the temple when they heard a shout.

"Amy! Dan! Stop!"

Amy whirled around. Pony was streaking toward them across the clearing, his ponytail flapping.

"Pony!" she called. "Get down!"

But he kept running. "The book's not here!" he shouted.

"Let's get out of here," Dan said.

They started back for the cover of the jungle. There was a sudden tearing noise near the temple as the tents burst open and out jumped three large, muscular men.

"Goons!" Dan cried. "Run!" They raced across the clearing for the jungle. But the trees shook in the windless night, and out of the shadows stepped more of Pierce's men, at least a dozen, blocking their way back to the hotel.

They were trapped. And this time there were more thugs to fight than ever.

CHAPTER 28

The men moved quickly. They were on Amy, Dan, and Pony in seconds.

Amy scanned the area for a way out, but they were surrounded. The soldiers backed them up against the ruined temple. There was nowhere to go but up. "This way!" She tugged on Pony and Dan to follow her as she scrambled up the unexcavated side of the pyramid, a huge mound of dirt with vines and ferns and trees growing out of it.

She could have reached the top of the temple way ahead of the soldiers, but she couldn't leave Dan and Pony behind. Dan was in great shape, but he couldn't compete with Amy — the serum had made her as fast as the fastest Olympic runner. Pony was a desk jockey, not used to running for his life. He slowed them both down.

The thugs quickly caught up with them. The sight of their bulging muscles and stone-cold eyes filled Amy with rage, and, as if in response, her muscles flooded with strength. One fighter went after the weak link, Pony, but Amy perched above him on the slippery side of the temple, which gave her an advantage. She kicked him square in the chest and the soldier tumbled off the pyramid. Amy grabbed Pony just before the men could drag him down.

"Thanks!" Pony said.

"Don't thank me," Amy said. "Get to the top while I fight them off!"

She kicked another thug off the temple, but as soon as one crashed to the ground, another climbed up. She glanced back. Dan and Pony had reached the top of the pyramid. Two soldiers were just beginning to climb back up the dirt mound, so she had a few seconds. She raced to the top, grabbed a vine, and tested it. It was solidly wound around the tall branch of a kapok tree standing twenty feet from the pyramid.

"Use this to slide down!" she told Dan and Pony. They wrapped their hands around the rough vine and slid from the top of the pyramid back to the jungle floor. They disappeared among the vegetation to wait for her.

The soldiers kept coming. Amy kicked one in the chest, her right foot landing clean and hard on his sternum. He flew backward with a yelp. She shifted to her left foot and knocked a second thug to the ground. But a third was climbing up right behind him. He grabbed one of her feet and jerked her off balance. She fell onto her back, her head nearly striking an exposed tree root.

The thug pounced on her, going for her neck. He gripped her throat so hard she couldn't breathe. Amy tore his hands off her neck and rocked back, lifting her legs. She drove both feet into his stomach, pushing him off. He tumbled down the mound.

She'd nearly been strangled, but she felt nothing, no pain, nothing but fierce energy. She jumped to her feet and quickly climbed down to find Dan and Pony.

Two soldiers were waiting for her in the brush. One gripped Pony by the ponytail, yanking his head back; the other dangled Dan by the scruff of his neck like a kitten about to be drowned. Pony's eyes were huge with terror. Dan kept kicking his captor in the shins, but the thug didn't seem to notice. "Let them go," Amy growled. They couldn't hold on to Pony and Dan and fight her at the same time. They dropped the boys and dove for her.

She jumped aside, evading them, then knocked each one out with a hard chop to the neck. She heard rustling in the bushes behind her.

"More coming. Run."

She felt almost animal, supernatural, like the Mayan gods she'd seen in carvings and drawings around Tikal. She was the Jaguar God when she ran, she struck lightning-fast like a serpent, she had the wits of a Jester God. She could have outrun the soldiers. But Dan and Pony couldn't keep up. She had no choice but to fight to protect them.

She tore through the jungle, dragging the boys behind her, looking for someplace safe for them to hide until she could fight off the army . . . *if* she could fight them all off. . . .

THE 39 CLUES

184

She shook this doubt away. She'd do it. She had to do it. She scanned the jungle while she ran. Fifty feet ahead, a ruined stone wall, about four feet high, glimmered in the moonlight. If they could get behind it, they could use it for cover and maybe lose the thugs long enough to get back to the hotel.

She pushed Dan and Pony over the wall.

"Amy, no." Dan immediately crawled back over the wall and stood beside her. "I'll fight with you."

"You can't." She shoved him back to the other side. "Take cover."

He pulled himself up to the top of the wall again. "I'm in charge, remember?"

"Yes," she said. "Just not right now."

"Amy," Pony pleaded. "Run for it. Save yourself."

"Pony's right," Dan said. "You can escape. Run for it. We'll take our chances."

They were willing to sacrifice themselves—for her. And it infuriated Amy. She saw how the fight looked through their eyes—like a losing battle. Twelve men against one girl. They didn't understand. She'd taken the serum. She could win this.

"When you see a chance, take Pony and run back to the hotel," she said to Dan with a note of finality in her voice. Dan might be the leader now. Her judgment might be faulty at times. But every cell in her body screamed, *Protect him!* And she couldn't ignore it.

She raced along the wall, fifty feet, a hundred, fast as lightning, leading the soldiers away from the boys.

Then she turned to face her attackers head on.

She used a judo throw to flip the first over her head. She neatly dodged the next, and a third. She grabbed a fallen tree branch to use as a weapon, fending the soldiers off as fast as she could. But they kept coming. Four of them, six, ten, twelve . . .

She was surrounded. She leaped up to the top of the wall, hoping the extra height would give her an advantage. She swung the branch at a fighter, toppling him like a bowling pin. *You can do this.*

And then it happened.

She felt a sudden weakness in her legs. She paused, gripping the branch-sword, but her hands shook like a tree in a storm. *No*, she thought desperately. *Not now.* The power drained from her limbs. Her eyes rolled back in her head. She felt herself sliding down the wall, the rough stone scraping her arms, dots swimming before her eyes. This episode was worse than before. Worse than anything she'd felt in her life.

"Amy! Amy!"

She could hear Dan calling her, but she couldn't see him. She couldn't see anything but dots and swirling colors. She knew what was happening. This time she knew: another hallucination. *This isn't real*, she thought. *I can't let it take over.* Then she heard screeches, terrible heart-ripping cries. *Howler monkeys*, she thought. *I'm surrounded by howler monkeys. Get them away from me!* They jumped up and down, then attacked her, grabbing at her hair and face with their hairy paws.

No! she screamed. *Stop it! Stop it! It's an illusion*, she thought. *Make it go away!* She summoned all her strength to clear her mind, to fight the darkness. She heard footsteps pounding toward her. Were they real? They came closer . . . closer . . . then attacked! Hands grabbed her arms. She flicked them away. The colors in her vision faded to black and gray. She felt as if she were staring through a soupy fog, at shadows, while the screaming filled her ears. Something tried to pick her up and carry her off—monkey? Man? She couldn't tell. She kicked blindly, her foot and knee hitting something hard until the something let her go.

Through the chaos and the noise, she heard Dan calling to her: "Amy! Help! Help!"

Dan. She had to help Dan. She kicked and punched at anything that touched her, scratching and clawing until, at last, the attacks stopped.

Everything went quiet. Her vision cleared, the fog melting away. The somethings were gone. Had they been howler monkeys, or men? She didn't know. She was standing by a ruined wall in the moonlight, alone.

"Dan!" she shouted. "Pony! Where are you?"

She heard shouting a little distance away. She ran back to the loggers' clearing. The noises grew louder. The *huff huff huff* of a chopper's blades whirred overhead. A black helicopter hovered over the clearing, preparing to land.

Two thugs, their faces scratched and bloody, grabbed her. Her strength surged again, and she knocked them to the ground where they remained, motionless.

The chopper blades whipped up a wind as it landed in the clearing, sending dirt and leaves flying. Amy shielded her face and backed away. Under the chopper, on the other side of it, she saw feet running toward the chopper door. She dashed across the clearing, ducking under the whirring rotors. *Dan!* Two soldiers were dragging him into the chopper. Another held Pony back as they shut Dan inside. Then he let Pony go and hurried into the chopper himself. Pierce's men were leaving, and they were taking Dan with them.

"Dan! No!" Amy screamed, and ran for the chopper. But Pony was closer. He dove for the landing skid, clutching it as the copter lifted off the ground.

"Pony! Let go!" Amy tried to leap into the air and grab the skid herself, but it was too high. The machine took off, Pony's legs dangling just out of her reach. She jumped as high as she could, but it wasn't enough.

The helicopter soared up over the trees, Pony clinging to the bottom. He was hanging on by his fingertips, his face pinched with the strain, his tongue poking out of his mouth in concentration. She could just make out Dan's frantic face pressed to the window, and behind him, a thug watching Pony and laughing. Amy held her breath. It was too late for Pony to let go now — the chopper was too high.

"Hang on!" she shouted. "Hang on!"

Pony's legs brushed the top of a tree. He tried to step on a branch, as if he might land there, but it wasn't solid enough. Amy thought she could see the muscles in his arms quivering, using all his strength.

Amy wanted to close her eyes, but she couldn't. She kept hoping a hand would reach out of the chopper door and pull Pony to safety, that some miracle would happen. . . . She found herself reaching for him, jumping up over and over as if she could spring into the air and save him.

But she was rooted to the ground, and he dangled in the sky, helpless.

One of his hands slipped off the skid. He hung on for his life by one sweaty hand.

The chopper lifted higher, far above the trees now. Pony strained his free hand toward the skid, trying to grab hold, but he couldn't reach it. His shoulder snapped out of position, dislocating.

And then the other hand slipped off. Down he fell.

Amy screamed as she watched his tiny figure drop from the sky and disappear among the trees. The chopper floated away.

The jungle went quiet.

Amy stood alone in the clearing. The chopper was gone. Dan was gone. Pony was surely dead.

She ran into the jungle, hoping for a miracle. Praying to find Pony alive.

She sped through the dense trees, jumping over obstacles and ripping at vines that blocked her way.

She must have run about a mile when she found him. Pony's body had landed on the branch of a tree, twenty feet overhead, his back arched at an unnatural angle, broken. His head hung back, his ponytail dangling, his mouth gaping, moonlight glowing in his open, glassy eyes.

Amy's legs buckled under her. She collapsed on the damp ground. The strength drained out of her now, leaving her nearly paralyzed.

Pony is dead. He's dead.

He died trying to save me.

And Dan is gone.

She was a failure. She had failed in every way.

Tears leaked out of her eyes. She couldn't stop them. She lay in the damp dirt and sobbed. She'd had all that power. The power of Gideon's serum. Unfathomable strength of body, mind, and will. And what good did it do her? The side effects were getting worse. She was declining every day. And yet, somehow, she had to find the superhuman power to get up. To rescue Dan. To keep going after the antidote. Because without it, they were all doomed.

She rested a little while longer until she felt some strength return to her legs. Then, as dawn broke, she hoisted herself to her feet and made her trudging, defeated, heartbroken way through the teeming jungle, back to the hotel.

She would break the news to the others. They would be horrified, and mourn. But they would summon their last scraps of will and continue the fight. There was nothing else to do.

ATTLEBORO CRIER

EARLY EDITION

HAIL TO THE CHIEF

By Logan Black

USA – J. Rutherford Pierce is days away from announcing his candidacy for president of the United States, heralding the beginning of a new age for America. The *Attleboro Crier* would like to announce our formal endorsement of this visionary leader who, for good reason, is already considered a front-runner. Don't let yourself end up on the wrong side of history. Pledge your support today! (For more info on the Pierce campaign, turn to any page in this paper, a proud

READ THE STORY p. 14